When Saul arrived to inherit the family home, Lucy was appalled to discover that the boy she had taunted as a child had become a very attractive man; a man, moreover, who did not show any signs of being able to forgive her for the past.

Books you will enjoy
by PENNY JORDAN

CAPABLE OF FEELING

Sophy had married Jon knowing she was safe from any sexual advances, because Jon was incapable of feeling anything but brotherly love for her. But now she was living with him, she began to wonder if that was the sort of love she really wanted from him . . .

DESIRE NEVER CHANGES

Rejected once by Chase, could Somer really face living with him? And why did he want to marry her, now, when she believed he had forgotten all about her?

A MAN POSSESSED

Kate knew that Dominic Harland was a man possessed with a desire to hurt her for what she had done in the past. How could he possibly want her at all?

RESEARCH INTO MARRIAGE

Jessica was sure that romantic love was a myth. She was even writing a book to prove it. And she was considering marrying Lyle Garnett to prove that arranged marriages were more successful than the ones based on love. So why did she react to Lyle the way she did?

RETURN MATCH

BY

PENNY JORDAN

MILLS & BOON LIMITED
15–16 BROOK'S MEWS
LONDON W1A 1DR

First published in Great Britain 1986
by Mills & Boon Limited

© Penny Jordan 1986

Australian copyright 1986
Philippine copyright 1986
This edition 1986

ISBN 0 263 75491 X

Set in Monophoto Plantin 11 on 11½ pt.
01–1086 – 47508

Printed and bound in Great Britain by
Collins, Glasgow

CHAPTER ONE

'BUT *why* do we have to move out of the Manor and into the Dower House?' six-year-old Tara protested stubbornly, the full lower lip so like their father's trembling ominously.

Across the tousled fair head Fanny gazed despairingly at her stepdaughter, and Lucy automatically suppressed her own tiredness and irritation.

'Tara, you know why,' she said patiently. 'Now that . . . Now that Daddy's . . . gone, we can't live here any longer. The house belongs to someone else now.'

It had been a long day—a long and wearying month in fact since her father's death from a third and long-dreaded heart attack, but then he had never learned to live quietly as his doctor had advised him—but beneath Tara's belligerence she sensed the six-year-old's fear at the way her small world was being destroyed, and it was this fear she sought to ease.

Ironic really that Tara should turn to her and not to her own mother, Lucy's stepmother Fanny, but then, as the late George Martin had known, Fanny was one of the weaker vessels of this life, not the stronger. Some of his last words to his elder daughter had been a warning that she was the one on whom the small family would now have to lean—not Fanny.

'It's not fair.' Another voice joined the chorus, the face of Fanny's ten-year-old son setting in lines of stubborn resentment, familiar to Lucy. 'If you had been a boy we needn't have lost the Manor. You could have inherited it.'

Repressing a sigh Lucy shook her head.

'The Manor has always been entailed to the closest male heir, Oliver,' she reminded her half-brother. 'You know that.'

'Yes.' The boy's gruff admission wrung her heart. Unwittingly her eyes met Fanny's and, reading the guilt and misery in them, slid quickly away. She felt like a conspirator involved in some dark and unseemly crime, and Fanny's attitude of guilty misery only served to heighten her feelings.

She wished more than she had wished anything in her life that her father had not chosen to burden her with his death-bed confessions; but he had, and in doing so had put on her shoulders a responsibility she was not sure she was able to carry.

The promise he had extracted from her to look after Fanny and the children, she could accept; but this other burden, this 'secret' that only she and Fanny shared . . .

Her mouth compressed slightly as she looked across the packing-case strewn room at Oliver. Up until just over a month ago she had believed Oliver to be Fanny's son from her first marriage to a local MP, but now she had been told that Oliver was in fact her father's child, conceived during an affair with Fanny which had begun while she was still married.

Her father had been quite free to marry Fanny,

but it seemed that Fanny had been unwilling to risk the shame of a divorce from her husband who at the time had been newly elected to Parliament.

In the event, Henry Willis had been the one to do the divorcing when *his* affair with his secretary became public knowledge, leaving her father and Fanny to marry after a decent interval of time had elapsed.

However, by then Oliver had been four years old, and once again rather than risk any scandal Fanny had insisted that he should continue to be thought Henry's child.

In a surge of bitterness during his last hours, her father had confided to her that it was a damn shame that Tara had not been the child to be born outside the marriage and Oliver within it, because then he would not have been put to the necessity of realising as many of his assets as possible to ensure that very little more than the Manor House itself should pass out of his family's hands.

Privately Lucy had been appalled when she learned what her father had done and if he had not been so dreadfully ill, she would have been tempted to point out to him that it was Fanny, rather than Saul Bradford, who had deprived Oliver of his birthright.

After the funeral, Fanny had come to her weeping copiously to plead with her never, ever to reveal the truth about Oliver. She could not endure the trauma of the scandal there would be if the truth were to come out, she had said tearfully, and Lucy had weakly agreed.

Privately, having had a long talk with her father's solicitor, she felt that, even if Oliver had inherited, within a very short space of time the Manor would have had to be sold. The roof was in need of repair, some of the windows needed attention, and it grieved her to walk through the once elegant rooms and see how shabby they had become.

It was far too large to be maintained as a private home, unless of course one was a millionaire, which her father had been far from being.

By anyone else's standards, the Georgian Dower House was a very elegant and spacious dwelling, and much, much more manageable. She herself, the eldest of her father's three children and the one who had lived in the Manor the longest, was the least reluctant to leave it. Perhaps because she had long ago outgrown childhood, and could see all too clearly the headaches attached to owning the Manor.

The oldest part of the house was Elizabethan, its pretty black and white frontage hiding a warren of passages and dark, tiny rooms with sloping floors.

A Stuart Martin had added the panelling and more imposing entrance hall with its Grinling Gibbons staircase, but it had been left to a Georgian ancestor to completely overshadow the original building by adding a complete wing and restructuring the grounds so that a fine carriageway swept round to an impressive portico in the centre of this new wing, leaving the Elizabethan part of the house as no more than a mere annexe to this fine new development.

Now damp, seeping in through the damaged roof, was causing mould to darken the fine plasterwork in the ballroom on the second floor, the creeping tide of deterioration so slow that it was not until quite recently, looking at the place through the eyes of her cousin Saul Bradford, that Lucy realised just how bad it was.

Really the house was more suitable for a hotel or conference centre than a private home, and she privately had little doubt that Saul would sell it just as soon as possible.

She remembered quite well from his one visit to the Manor how derogatory and contemptuous he had been of her home. They had met only once—over twelve years ago now, and the meeting had not been a success.

She had found him brash and alien, and no doubt he had found her equally alien and unappealing. They had neither of them made allowances for the other. She had still been getting over the shock of her mother's death in a riding accident—she had always been closer to her mother than her father—and Saul, although she hadn't known it, had been sent to them by *his* mother so that he would be out of the way while she and his father fought out a particularly acrimonious divorce.

She sighed faintly, grimacing inwardly. It was too late now to regret the various snubs and slights she had inflicted on a raw and unfriendly American boy all those years ago, but she did regret them and had for quite some time—not because Saul was her father's heir, but simply because with maturity had come the realisation that Saul had been as hurt and in need of comfort as she had herself and it grieved her to acknowledge that she had allowed herself to be influenced in her manner towards him by someone who she now recognised as a vindictive cruel human being.

At twelve she had not been able to see this, and in fact had been held fast in the toils of a mammoth crush on her cousin Neville.

Still, it was too late for regrets now, but not too late hopefully to make amends. Despite the antipathy her father had felt towards Saul, and which he seemed to have passed on to his son and widow, Lucy was determined to make life as uncomplicated as she possibly could for her American cousin and to give him whatever help he needed.

It was not as though, by inheriting, he had deprived her of anything after all—she had known very early on in life that the Manor was entailed; but Oliver, whom her father had spoilt dreadfully, seemed to be finding it difficult to adjust.

Privately Lucy thought the adjustment would do him no harm at all. In the last couple of years she had begun to detect signs in him that her father's spoiling and his mother's complete inability to institute any form of discipline were changing him from a pleasingly self-confident little boy into an unpleasant, self-centred pre-teenager.

Fortunately she was fond enough of her half-brother and sister for her father's charge that she look after them not to be too onerous a burden.

Fanny, however, was another matter. Although they got on well enough, there were times when Lucy found it exasperating to have a stepmother who behaved more like a dependent child.

'I don't want to go to the Dower House.'

Tara's bottom lip wobbled again, tears glistening in the dark brown eyes.

Physically both Tara and herself took after their father's family, Lucy thought, eyeing her half-sister sympathetically. Both of them had the deep brown Martin eyes and strikingly contrasting blonde hair. And the elegant profile, which family rumour said had led to an eighteenth-century Amelia Martin being propositioned by the Prince Regent. It was because she had turned him down that the family had never received a title, or so the family story went, but how much truth there was in it, Lucy did not know. Perhaps, when she had researched a little more of the family's history, she might find out.

Eighteen months ago she had started to sift through the family papers, trying to make some order of them, and it was then that she had first conceived the idea of writing a novel based loosely on her family's history. Now, that one novel was threatening to develop into three or four, and next week in fact she was due to go to London to talk about this possibility with the publishers who had expressed an interest in her initial manuscript.

She had been lucky there—there was no doubt about that; her mother's family had connections in the publishing world. Her cousin Neville was a partner in a firm of publishers—not the one she was dealing with, but his father had made the recommendation for her, much to Neville's disgust; he was no doubt hoping she would fall flat on her face, if she knew Neville, Lucy thought wryly.

She had got over her crush on her cousin many years ago, and all that was left was a healthy wariness of the man he had become. Occasionally he indulged himself in light-hearted flirtatiousness with her—more to see exactly how vulnerable she might be to him than for any other reason. Neville was extremely conceited and never liked losing an admirer. His father and her mother had been brother and sister, and Lucy retained a deep fondness for her uncle and his wife.

'Tara, please stop that noise . . . My head . . .'

Fanny's protest broke through her reverie, making her realise that Tara was crying in earnest now, while Oliver scowled and kicked disconsolately at one of the packing cases and Fanny pressed a fragile hand to her forehead.

'Lucy, I must go and lie down . . . My poor head . . .'

Knowing that she would make faster progress with her stepmother out of the way Lucy made no demur, summoning a smile and a few words of sympathy, while at the same time producing a handkerchief for Tara's tears and warning Oliver not to ruin his shoes.

'Come on, it won't be that bad,' she comforted Tara when Fanny had gone to her room. 'You'll like the Dower House.'

'Yes, but what about Harriet?'

Harriet was Tara's exceedingly plump little pony, and for a moment Lucy frowned, not following the thread of her half-sister's conversation.

'Well I'm sure Harriet will like it, too,' she told her. 'She will have that lovely paddock all to herself.'

'But Richard says that we won't be able to keep her. That you won't be able to afford it . . .'

Richard was the junior partner in her father's firm of solicitors and Lucy frowned at the mention of his name. For several months now he had been making it plain that he wanted more from her than the casual relationship they presently enjoyed.

Only the other week he had mentioned marriage, adding that the fact that her father had left the Dower House to Lucy in her sole name would mean that on marriage she would have a very comfortable home to share with her husband.

The reason her father had left the house to her was that he didn't want any gossip to arise from the fact that he was leaving the bulk of the money he had realised, from selling everything that wasn't entailed, in trust for Oliver and Tara, with the income to go to Fanny until the children reached their majority. Lucy had been less than impressed that Richard should choose to mention marriage only when he realised what her father had left her.

She wondered if Richard was also aware that she had as good as promised her father that both children and Fanny would have a home with her as long as they needed it. Richard did not like children, and neither Oliver nor Tara liked him. Anyway there was not the remotest possibility of her marrying him. To put it bluntly, sexually he left her stone-cold. As did most men. So much so that she had reached the grand old age of twenty-five without a single passionate affair to look back on. Was that the fault of her lifestyle or her genes?

There had been a time, just before her father married Fanny, when she had made a bid for freedom, suggesting that she leave the newly married couple alone and move to London, but Fanny had pleaded with her to stay.

Almost from the moment of her mother's death Lucy had run the house—not through choice but through necessity—and Fanny had claimed that the thought of taking over from her totally overwhelmed her. And so, despite her misgivings, she had stayed, trying not to feel too guilty about the waste of a perfectly good degree and the loss of her personal independence.

Since then her life had been busy rather than fulfilling. There were certain responsibilities incumbent on living in the Manor, certain local charities her mother had taken an interest in and helped, and this mantle had now fallen to her.

Her decision to try and write had been born of the mental starvation she suffered from, Lucy suspected, and certainly the hours she spent alone in the library on her research had been among the most fulfilling she had experienced since leaving university.

Now, though, she was likely to lose all that, unless Saul allowed her to use the library.

He was such an unknown quantity, she wasn't really sure what to expect. Her memories of him were clouded by the animosity which had sprung up between them almost from the word go and when she pictured him mentally, it was with a truculent scowl on his face.

In looks he didn't resemble the Martins at all, being very dark, almost swarthily so, his eyes grey and not brown, his transatlantic accent adding to his alienness.

Looking back on that disastrous summer, Lucy felt a twinge of sympathy towards him.

Poor boy, it couldn't have been easy for him—thrown upon relatives he did not know, who moreover spoke differently and had a different set of rules to live by. That scowl, that stubborn indifference to all that the Manor had to offer, must have been defensive rather than aggressive, but of course at twelve she could not see that, and had only seen that he mocked everything that she held dear, while all the time reinforcing his own Americanness. The brash superiority had just increased her own dislike of him, so that she had willingly joined Neville in his tormenting of him.

Neville . . . so smooth and sophisticated to her then, so excitingly male and aloof, and yet undeniably a part of her world in a way that the American intruder was not. When Neville spoke, it was in the same way as her father, his accent public school and clipped, unlike Saul's American drawl.

Even the way he dressed was different . . . alien

. . . And how she and Neville had tormented him when they watched the way he rode! She had been unkind almost to the point of being cruel and had since regretted it deeply because it was not part of her nature to inflict hurt on others.

Poor Saul. How did *he* remember her? she wondered wryly. Well, she would have ample opportunity to make restitution for her sins once he arrived. Neville might speak slightingly of the Manor passing into American hands, but now she did not encourage him.

Tara had stopped crying and was watching her hopefully. 'We won't be too poor to keep Harriet,' she told her firmly. 'Richard was quite wrong.'

'Are you going to marry him?'

That was Oliver, eyeing her truculently.

'No.'

Relief showed briefly in the brown eyes before he turned away. Oliver had been closer to their father than any of them, something she had not really thought about before she knew the truth, and Oliver was the one who would miss his male influence the most. Perhaps Saul might be induced to take an interest in him. Perhaps he was married now with children of his own.

It was a shock to realise how little she knew about him. In all the anxiety and tumult of her father's death, she had had little time to spare to wonder about Saul; little time to give to him at all apart from overseeing the sending of a telegram to advise him of what had happened.

She had half hoped he would attend the funeral and had been almost hurt when he had not.

Towards the end her father had complained that Saul had never made the slightest attempt to learn anything about his heritage, but fair-mindedly Lucy had pointed out that he had scarcely been given much chance.

Certainly her own memories of Saul weren't happy ones, but like her he had no doubt matured and mellowed, and probably also, like her, knowing the close proximity to one another in which they would be living, he would want their relationship to be an amicable one.

Despite all these sensible thoughts Lucy could not quite stifle the apprehension burgeoning to life inside her. As yet they had no idea when Saul would arrive, but she was being meticulous about vacating the Manor just as quickly as she could. She was also being meticulous about what she took with her—only the furniture which had been her mother's and nothing more.

Fortunately the Dower House was furnished, although somewhat haphazardly as up until quite recently it had been tenanted, but no doubt the furniture that had been her mother's would make it seem more like home.

With the help of Mrs Isaacs, their daily, Lucy had already cleaned the house from top to bottom. Nearly all the rooms needed redecorating and she had promised herself that this was a task she would tackle just as soon as she had time. With the income from the trust funds her father had established for Oliver and Tara they would be able to manage financially—just about. Oliver's school fees would take a large slice of these funds, but Fanny had been adamant that her son must go to prep school at the start of the new term, as had been planned.

The school which had been chosen was George Martin's old school, and even though privately Lucy thought it was almost an extravagance to pay out such a large sum of money annually just so that Oliver could be educated at her father's old school, she had not had the heart to oppose Fanny.

It was her opinion that of the two of them Tara was the cleverer and inwardly she was determined that when the time came Tara would somehow be given the same opportunities as her brother. Fortunately at the moment that was one problem which could be shelved, unlike the jumble of packing cases now littering the ballroom floor.

She and Mrs Isaacs had brought them here mainly because of the large area of empty floor space, and tomorrow morning Mr Isaacs and his two large sons were going to drive up from the village with their van and spend the day transporting the cases over to the Dower House.

From the ballroom window it was possible to look right across the park that surrounded the house and Lucy caught her lip between her teeth as she glanced at the view. They had almost the same view from the Dower House, which was surrounded by a very pleasant garden.

With hindsight Lucy could recognise that her father's decision to divorce the Dower House and a certain amount of land from the main house had probably originated with Oliver's birth; even then he must have been planning to do everything he could for his illegitimate child, she

thought wryly. But, in doing so, there was no
getting away from the fact that he had stripped
the Manor of anything that might usefully have
been sold to provide its new owner with funds.
The farmlands had now all gone, the last few
acres having been sold just prior to her father's
death.

Those paintings which had not been sold
previously to cover death duties had been
auctioned at Sotheby's eighteen months ago,
along with the few good antiques they had left.

Now the house had a forlorn, neglected air,
almost an air of desolation and desertion. What
on earth Saul would do with the place she had no
idea. Sell it most likely; she could not see how he
could do anything else.

Sighing faintly she turned away from the view
and surveyed the packing cases. She had written
in chalk on each one what it contained,
meticulously refusing to pack the Meissen dinner
service or what was left of the family silver.
Those went with the house and she was
determined that they would stay with it.

Whatever wealth the Martin family had once
possessed from trade and a sugar planation in the
West Indies had been dissipated by the time of
the First World War, and since then the family
had survived by gradually selling off its assets. It
was true that her father had held several
directorships which had brought in a reasonable
income, but the house simply devoured money.

The same Martin who had added the Georgian
frontage to the house had also commissioned the
Dower House, and its Georgian elegance had

always appealed to Lucy. She knew their solicitor found it strange that it had been left to her and not to Fanny, but Lucy understood the reason why.

Her father had thought that the security of the family would be safer in her hands than Fanny's and indeed her stepmother was, in some ways, very much another child. She had leaned on George Martin during their marriage and Lucy suspected that now she would lean on her.

Fanny didn't really care for the country and spent as much time as she could in London, staying with friends. Neither was she particularly maternal, allowing Lucy to take day-to-day charge of her half-brother and sister. Fortunately the three of them got on well together, but it was typical of Fanny's nature that she should not consider that a single woman of twenty-five might not want the responsibility for a stepmother and two children.

The one thing she would miss about the Manor was the library, Lucy reflected half an hour later as she went downstairs. Her book, although fiction, relied heavily on information she had discovered among the family papers and diaries and she was hoping that Saul would allow her to use these for her work. She could of course simply take them and he would be none the wiser, but her own strict code of ethics would not allow her to do that. The unhappy, shy teenager, who had allowed her older male cousin to bully her into being unkind to their colonial relative, had long since been superseded by a woman who knew her own mind and how to stick to her own decisions and assessments.

She grimaced faintly as she stepped into the kitchen. This was one room she would not miss. Large and old-fashioned, it was ill-lit and ill-equipped, unlike the kitchen at the Dower House which had been installed by one of their tenants.

After her father's death, in an attempt to cut back on costs, Lucy had been obliged to let Mrs Jennings, who had acted as their cook-cum-housekeeper, go. She had been eager to retire and more than happy with the generous cheque Lucy had given her, but Fanny had not stopped grumbling, complaining that it was too much to expect her to provide meals for all of them.

Because of this Lucy had discovered that she was the one doing the cooking, something which in other circumstances she might not have minded, but which in addition to all her other responsibilities had the effect of making her heart sink every time she entered the kitchen.

Tonight they would have to make do with beans on toast, she decided ruefully, anticipating Oliver's objections to this meagre fare. Tomorrow night she would make it up to them, she decided, but for tonight a snack would have to do. She wanted an early start in the morning and was already far too tired to start preparing a large meal.

This physical and mental exhaustion was something which seemed to have dogged her since her father's death, exacerbated by the discovery of Oliver's true parentage. In many ways it shocked her that her father should have been so imprudent, and what of Oliver himself? Telling herself that now was not the time to start worrying about the future, she started laying the table.

Tara came in just as she was finished.

'Mummy says she's got a headache,' she informed Lucy, 'and she wants to have her supper in her room.'

Stifling the exasperated sound springing to her lips, Lucy said nothing. She tried to be patient with Fanny, telling herself that after all her stepmother had lost a husband, while she had merely lost a father who had not been particularly close to her. She could still remember the acute devastation of losing her mother, whom she had truly loved, and if Fanny was experiencing just one tenth of the anguish she had experienced then, then she did indeed deserve her sympathy and patience.

Fanny wouldn't want beans on toast anyway. Perhaps if she boiled her a couple of eggs . . .

'Go and tell Oliver to wash his hands and come down to eat, will you, Tara?' she instructed the younger girl. 'I want you both to have an early night tonight because we've got a lot to do tomorrow.'

'Yes. I've already told Harriet all about her new paddock,' Tara responded importantly. 'Do you think she'll really like it there, Lucy? She'll miss Cinders, won't she?'

Cinders was the small tabby cat who lived in the dilapidated stables; suppressing a smile, Lucy said seriously, 'Oh, I think we can take Cinders with us.'

'But you said that we couldn't take anything that belonged to the Manor.'

So she had, but privately Lucy could not see that her cousin was going to object too much to the removal of one small cat, and, as Tara had said, her pony was very attached to the little animal.

'Is he really horrid, Lucy?'

'Horrid? Who?'

She turned away from what she was doing, her attention concentrated on the little girl.

'Your cousin. The one who's coming to live here.'

'Good heavens, of course he isn't horrid. Whatever gave you that idea?' Heavens! The very last thing she wanted was for the children to take an anti towards Saul, and she had better nip that idea of Tara's very firmly in the bud.

'Oliver said he was,' Tara told her determinedly, 'and Neville told him.'

Mentally cursing her maternal cousin, Lucy said airily, 'Oh I expect Neville was just joking. I promise you Saul is very nice.'

Behind her back she crossed her fingers. Tara's scowl relaxed. 'And he won't take Harriet away from me?'

'Of course not. Now go and tell Oliver to come down for supper.'

CHAPTER TWO

IT was another three very hectic days before they were able to actually move into the Dower House, and as she surveyed the now empty ballroom Lucy reflected that she was more tired than she had ever felt in her life.

Fanny had alternated between bouts of weeping, shutting herself away in her bedroom, and an almost frenzied desire to have her children beside her.

Both of them were unsettled by their mother's half-hysterical behaviour, especially Tara, but, now that they had actually physically left the Manor, Lucy was hoping that Fanny would start to make a recovery.

An odd kind of melancholy engulfed her as she wandered through the familiar rooms, stopping every now and again to touch some familiar item of furniture. She loved the old house, but felt no possessive desire to live in it. She had grown up after all knowing that it was entailed and would never be hers. A small smile curled her mouth as she thought back over the years, remembering that Neville had been more upset than she was herself when her father had curtly explained to both of them what the entail involved.

That had been the year before Saul had spent the summer with them. Up until then Neville had always claimed that when they grew up he intended to marry her. Even as a child Neville had had a keen eye for the main chance, she thought, wryly amused that she could ever have been taken in by her cousin's shallowness.

How long would it be before Saul arrived? A familiar sliver of tension spasmed through her stomach and she pushed it aside, annoyed with herself. What was there to feel apprehensive about? Her ownership of the Dower House was secure enough after all and, even if he wished to do so, Saul could not dislodge her. But why should he want to? The fact that they had not got on as children could hardly influence his attitude towards her now . . . could it?

It was disconcerting to realise how little she knew about him. Her aunt, his mother, had left home just after the war to marry her American. Much against their parents' wishes, her mother had told her once when Lucy had pressed her for more information about her aunt who lived so far away.

About Saul's father she knew very little, only that his mother had divorced him. It struck her uncomfortably that her father had been rather remiss in not making any attempt to get to know the nephew who would succeed him, but, knowing her father as she had done, Lucy recognised that he had probably hoped right up until the end that somehow he would be able to prevent the inevitable and pass the Manor on to Oliver.

In his own way her father had been as much of an ostrich as Fanny. Still, it was too late to regret her father's omissions now. Even to her accustomed eyes, the house looked shabby. She hoped that Saul wasn't expecting too much of his inheritance. She remembered he had not allowed himself to be overly impressed with it on his one visit, grimly ignoring all her heavily embellished boastings about secret stairways and haunted rooms.

As she walked past the giltwood mirror over the drawing-room fireplace she saw that her face was streaked with dust, her hair curling wildly about her face. Her hands and clothes were filthy, too. She needed a bath. There was nothing left for her to do here apart from locking up. Tomorrow she and Mrs Isaacs could set about cleaning the place properly.

As she slipped out into the courtyard at the back of the house she remembered that she had promised to feed Harriet, who was still in her stable. They had been too busy as yet to take her down to her new home in the paddock. Thank goodness it was summer and they would have time to build her a new stable in the paddock before winter came.

The fat little pony whickered a greeting as Lucy opened her door, Cinders winding herself sinuously round her ankles. She dealt quickly with the feed before wandering disconsolately back to the Dower House.

The next morning she was awake early, disturbed by the unfamiliar pattern of the sunlight across her face. Groggily she opened her eyes and then winced as her stiff muscles made their protest. At least here in the Dower House she would not have to coax a sulky range into life before she could have any breakfast.

It was too early to wake the others and, once showered and downstairs, Lucy found herself enjoying the unfamiliar solitude. The kitchen, so airy and well equipped after the Manor's, made her spirits lift slightly, and as she sipped her fragrant hot coffee she went over her plans for the day. She had arranged to meet Mrs Isaacs up at the Manor at nine, which meant that for once Fanny would have to get the children's breakfast. Shrugging away a faint feeling of guilt, she reminded herself that after all Fanny was their mother.

By eleven o'clock the clean jeans and T-shirt she had come out in were streaked with dust and grime. Her skin felt hot and sticky, her body was aching.

'I think we'll take a break,' she suggested to Mrs Isaacs.

'A good idea. I'll go down and make us both a cup of tea.'

Mrs Isaacs had been gone for about five minutes when Lucy heard the car, the shock of the unexpected sound drawing her to the window.

It was a large BMW, and it was stopping right outside the front of the house. A tremor of nerves seized her stomach as she watched the tall, dark-haired man emerge from the driver's seat.

Saul! Funny that she should recognise him so immediately when for weeks she had tried to conjure up his boyhood features without success.

He was wearing a lightweight pale grey suit

and looked, if anything, more European than American; dark enough to pass for an Italian, although perhaps rather too tall.

As she watched, Lucy saw Tara emerge from the side of the house, leading Harriet. The little girl was talking earnestly to the pony, who seemed oblivious to her mistress's attempts to get her to hurry. In fact Harriet seemed more interested in the juicy grass beside the drive than Tara's commands.

Lucy saw Saul move warily towards the little girl, the face which had seemed almost grim as he got out of the car softening slightly.

Tara had frozen at the sight of him, clinging desperately to Harriet's reins. Amused, Lucy watched as Saul's attempts to make friends were fiercely rebuffed, amusement changing to alarm as she realised that Tara was starting to cry. What on earth had Saul said to her?

Quickly she ran downstairs and out on to the drive, just in time to hear Tara crying out tearfully, 'You *are* horrid after all. Very horrid!'

Saul's hands were on Harriet's bridle, and Tara was desperately trying to tug the pony away.

As she saw Saul's face change, Lucy bit her lip. Now, with the amusement gone from his eyes, he looked very cold and alien.

Neither he nor Tara was aware of her until she called out sharply, 'Tara, that's enough.'

Tears flooded the brown eyes as they met Lucy's.

'Well he is,' Tara insisted stubbornly. 'You said he was nice, but he isn't.'

Saul was looking at her now, and Lucy felt the colour burn up under her skin as she realised what a dreadful picture she must present, her face stained with dust and completely free of make-up, her hair all tangled and untidy.

'Saul! How lovely to see you.' Ignoring Tara for the moment, she forced herself to smile the poised, self-confident smile she had learned so carefully, but it faded quickly when she realised he wasn't smiling back at her, his eyes as cold and grey as the North Sea as he looked her up and down and then without a word turned back to Tara.

'I wasn't really trying to take your pony away, you know,' he told her. 'I was just trying to make friends with her, that's all. She's far too small for me, but she reminds me of a pony I had when I was a little boy.'

Amazingly Tara stopped crying, her eyes widening as she whispered, 'Did you?'

'Yup. He lived on my uncle's farm, and I used to visit him during my vacations.'

His voice hadn't lost the soft drawl she remembered so vividly. Why on earth had she and Neville made fun of it? It was pleasantly soft and fell easily on her ears, causing her to suffer a momentary pang for her own folly in antagonising him. Instinctively she recognised now that he would have made a far better ally than Neville, that he could even have been a refuge for her to lean on during those difficult months after her mother's death.

Cross with herself for letting emotion get in the way of reality, she interrupted breathlessly. 'I'm sure Saul doesn't mind you taking your pony Tara . . .'

'Why should I?' he interrupted her in that same slow drawl. 'After all, you've already taken damned near everything else. What's a pony?'

The way he looked at her, the ironic contempt in his voice, stunned her into dismayed silence.

This was not what she had expected at all, this gage flung down at her feet for her to pick up. But what on earth could she say to him in her own defence?

She glanced at Tara. 'Take Harriet down to the paddock, Tara, and tell your mother that Saul's arrived.

'We didn't expect you quite so soon, and I'm afraid everything's still rather a mess. However, we'd be delighted if you'd have lunch with us.'

'My, my . . . how you've changed.' Again that biting mockery. 'Or have you? Those are very pretty party manners you've got somewhere along the way, Lucy. You certainly didn't have them twelve years ago.'

His cynicism stung her into replying fiercely, 'Twelve years ago I was still a child, Saul . . . And what's more I had just lost my mother.'

Watching his eyes harden she bit her lip, angry with herself for being so easily provoked. What on earth had happened to all her good resolutions about proferring an olive branch?

Turning away from him to hide the hot tide of colour flooding her skin from his penetrating glance, she mentally derided herself for the sensations engulfing her.

The truth was that she had stupidly expected a

more physically adult version of the boy Saul she had remembered, but what she had got was a man who seemed to share nothing other than a name with that boy she remembered.

'I want you to have lunch with us,' Tara interrupted firmly, gazing up at him. 'I want you to tell me all about your pony. What was his name?'

'Mustard.'

For some reason the slow smile he gave Tara made Lucy feel bleakly excluded and hurt.

'You're sure it's no trouble?'

He was looking at her now, his eyes still cold, smoothly assessing the shape of her body beneath its covering of skimpy T-shirt and ancient jeans, Lucy recognised. Anger flared hotly inside her, her mouth hardening as she turned away from him. As she fought for self-control she reminded herself that Saul had good reason to feel antagonistic towards her; he would after all have based his assessment of her on the girl she had been at twelve, and she could not really blame him for looking for chinks in her armour. Even so, in some strange way it hurt that he should have looked at her like that, dismissing the blood relationship between them, to treat her with a sexual contempt which she had found shatteringly demeaning.

Forcing a smile and ignoring the look he had given her she said calmly, 'No trouble at all. It will be about an hour or so before it's ready, but if you like I'll introduce you to Mrs Isaacs before I go. She and I have just been trying to clean the place up a bit.'

She just caught the look of surprise in his eyes
before he suppressed it and suddenly he looked
more like the boy she remembered.

'Rather a demeaning role for you isn't it?
Cleaning? Or were you hoping for a few more
pickings?'

A sense of despair engulfed her as she heard
the contempt in his voice. How could she have
thought that she simply had to extend to him the
hand of friendship to wipe out the past? Saul
might have left behind the awkward aggression
she remembered, but in its place was something
far more lethal: a cold hardness that warned her
that in his eyes she was more foe than friend.

'If you're referring to the estate,' she told him
quietly, 'my father was entitled to sell what he
did.'

She wasn't going to add that privately she had
not been in agreement with her father's actions,
but without raising her voice she added signifi-
cantly, 'He did after all have certain responsibilities.'

Saul looked at Tara and then equally softly told
her, 'In the last few months of his life your father
raised almost two hundred thousand pounds from
selling off everything that was unentailed—that's
an awful lot of money to support one widow and
her child . . . Or are you telling me that you're
included in those responsibilities? Hasn't anyone
ever told you about the pleasure of being self-
supporting, Lucy?'

She could feel her face sting, but even if Tara
had not been looking on there was no defence she
could honourably make. How could she tell him

of her promise to her father to keep the family together, to look after not only the children but Fanny as well?

'I'll take you to meet Mrs Isaacs.'

She caught the flash of bitterness in his eyes as she refused to respond to his barb, but what else could she do? She had not realised how bitter he would be about her father's actions, but without betraying the secret of Oliver's birth there was nothing she could do.

She maintained a cool distance while she introduced him to Mrs Isaacs, hesitating before offering to show him round the house. Mrs Isaacs was a warm-hearted soul, but a devout gossip, and she didn't want it to get round the village that there was bad feeling between herself and Saul, which would be the conclusion Mrs Isaacs was bound to leap to if she did not make the offer.

'I think I remember the layout pretty well. And I do have the plans so I don't think I'll get into too much trouble. Thanks for the offer though.'

He was dismissing her, Lucy thought irately; making it plain that he had no desire whatsoever for her company—or her presence in what was now his house.

'I'll see you at lunch time then.' Try as she might she could not quite keep the corresponding stiffness out of her own voice, and as he dipped his head in acknowledgment she recognised that he was entitled to the mockingly victorious smile that twisted his mouth.

As she had half expected, when she got back to the Dower House Fanny was still in bed. She wondered what the children had had for breakfast.

Concealing her exasperation, Lucy went up to warn her about their visitor.

'What's he like?'

'Tall dark and handsome,' Lucy responded flippantly, and then realised that it was quite true; and more than that there was a masculine strength about him that she found inordinately appealing.

Appealing? Nonsense! She was letting the fact that the responsibility for Fanny and the children weighed heavily on her shoulders get to her.

It took her almost half an hour to persuade Fanny that she ought to join them for lunch.

'You'll have to meet him sooner or later,' she reminded her stepmother. You don't want people to talk.'

It was a good ploy and one that brought a petulant frown to her stepmother's forehead.

'How on earth are we going to feed him, Lucy?' she demanded. 'These Americans are used to eating well, you know.'

'And so he will,' Lucy responded tartly. 'We're having asparagus from the garden, fresh salmon, and strawberries and cream.'

The salmon had been a gift from one of their neighbours, a retired colonel who had been a close friend of her father and who lived alone.

'I suppose the salmon was from Tom Bishop?' Fanny shook her head. 'That poor man. You know, he really should marry again Lucy . . . Living all alone in that huge house, spending all his time fishing . . .'

*　　*　　*

At one o'clock on the dot Saul rapped on the front door. Lucy, who had been working non-stop from the moment she walked in the house, determined that there was no way he was going to be able to look as slightingly on her meal as he had done on her person, paused in the hallway and then called to Tara to let him in.

'Take him into the drawing-room to your mother,' she instructed the little girl, 'and then go and tell Oliver to come downstairs.' Oliver was in his bedroom, organising his possessions.

She had been so busy she hadn't even had time to change, but now, from the safety of the kitchen where she was checking on the light sauce she had made to go with the salmon, she heard the drawing-room door and judged it was safe to dash upstairs and do something about her appearance.

Her wardrobe wasn't exactly bursting with fashionable clothes, her lifestyle didn't require them, but the few clothes she did have were good, carefully chosen and well cared for. Before her death her mother had once remarked approvingly that Lucy had inherited her own eye for colour and design, and the dress she hurriedly selected, a soft wrap-over style in pastel hued silk with pleats falling from the hip, was both elegant and feminine.

The soft peachy pink fabric with its pattern of muted greys and blues emphasised her summer tan, at once making her hair seem fairer and her eyes darker.

There was no time for her to bother with make-up and, quickly running a brush through her shoulder-length hair, she slipped on a pair of high-heeled sandals and hurried out of her room, almost colliding with Oliver at the top of the stairs.

He was, she saw with a sinking heart, looking oppressively sulky, his expression so like her father's that she wondered that she had never realised the truth.

'What's wrong?'

He glowered at her. 'I don't want any lunch . . . I don't want to have to talk to him . . . I don't want him here, Lucy.'

'Maybe not, but he is here and he has every right to be here,' she said as lightly as she could. 'Oliver, I do understand how you feel, but you must try to realise how he feels as well. You don't want everyone to think you resent the fact that he's inherited the Manor do you?'

He shook his head slowly 'I suppose not.'

'Good. Now come down and have your lunch. It's salmon. The colonel gave it to us.'

'Did he?' His face lit up. 'I wish I'd been there when he came. He might have told me some more about during the war.'

Lucy laughed, relieved to see his sulks banished.

'Well, there'll be plenty more opportunities to talk to him I'm sure.' Deliberately she didn't let him go into the drawing-room alone, propelling him slightly ahead of her as she opened the door.

Fanny was sitting in one of the armchairs facing the french windows and to her astonishment Saul was standing close beside her, one arm casually draped over Tara's shoulder as they all looked at something on her knee.

'Oh there you are, Lucy dear ...' Fanny looked slightly flustered. 'I was just showing Saul the photographs of our wedding. How pretty you look. It isn't often we see you in a dress. That must be for your benefit, Saul.' She smiled coyly up at him, blushing a little, while Lucy mentally seethed. She knew her stepmother to be completely innocent of any charge of guile, but nevertheless it was extremly galling that Saul should think she had dressed especially for him.

'Well I could hrdly sit down to lunch in my work clothes,' was all she said, but she was conscious of the mocking scrutiny in Saul's eyes as she crossed the room with Oliver, and introduced him to the older man.

She was pleased to see that instead of talking down to him Saul shook hands with the boy, gravely treating him very much as the man of the house. Oliver visibly relaxed and Lucy gave a mental sigh of relief. Oliver could be extremely intractable and sulky when he chose—the result of too much laxity and spoiling, which she tried to counteract as best she could, all too conscious that once Oliver went away to school he would find that discipline was imposed upon him whether he liked it or not. Here again she blamed her father for not taking a firmer hand and not realising what a traumatic shock it could be for Oliver to go straight from his mother's spoiling to the rigours of boarding school.

'Darling, I think we'd better go into the dining-room for lunch.' Fanny suggested. 'Will you bring it in?'

It was good to see Fanny rallying from her
depression and taking an interest in something
once more and Lucy willingly complied, leaving
the others to make their way to the dining-room
while she hurried to the kitchen.

Everyone was seated when she went in with the
asparagus.

The furniture in this room had been her
mother's, and if the Sheraton dining chairs were
rather scratched and worn, they were still
undeniably elegant.

'Asparagus . . . Very English,' Saul commented
as Lucy served him. 'From here?'

'From the Dower House's garden, yes,' she
agreed, making it plain to him that the asparagus
was not from the Manor. In point of fact the
vegetable garden attached to the Dower House
was better stocked and cared for—a legacy from
one of their tenants who had been a keen
gardener.

She had the satisfaction of seeing the faint tide
of colour creep up under his skin as he digested
her remark.

'Lucy, really,' Fanny reproached her. 'There's
no need for that. I'm sure that Saul wouldn't
have minded in the least had the asparagus come
from the Manor.'

The smile she directed towards him was one
she had always used to good effect on her
husband, and, watching Saul respond to it, Lucy
wondered a little bleakly if she herself wouldn't
be well advised to adopt a few feminine wiles.

Not once had Saul smiled at her like that. Not
once had he smiled at her at all.

'This is really delicious.'

He was looking at Fanny, who coloured modestly but said nothing.

Oliver, seated beside Lucy, frowned watching the by-play and then said sturdily, 'Mum didn't cook it—Lucy does all the cooking.'

She was aware of Saul looking at her, but refused to look back, concentrating on her food until she felt the concentration of his gaze slacken.

Fanny she saw was frowning slightly, not pleased by her son's comment. 'Poor Lucy has had to take charge of so much,' she told Saul, giving her stepdaughter a little smile. 'I'm afraid I've been so prostrate with misery that I haven't been able to do a thing.'

For a moment Lucy had to stifle a wild desire to remind her stepmother that never once since the start of her marriage had she shown the slightest interest in running the Manor, but she stifled it at birth, telling herself that she was being unfair. Fanny was Fanny and that was that.

'I'll go and get the main course,' she said calmly instead, quickly collecting the plates and heading for the door.

Saul reached it before her, his forearm touching her body as he leaned across her to open the door.

A *frisson* of sensation shivered through her, so unexpected as to be faintly shocking, and she drew back from him as though her skin burned.

'Am I correct in thinking I recognise the Sheraton?'

No one else could overhear the remark because

Saul had his back to the room and she was almost through the door.

. 'Yes,' she agreed curtly. 'It belonged to my mother and she willed it to me.'

There! Let him make what he liked of that!

The remainder of the meal passed all too slowly for Lucy. She was aware of Saul and Fanny conversing, but made no attempt to take part in their conversation. Saul praised the salmon and its accompanying sauce, looking at her this time, but she made no response. His remark about the furniture still hurt. Hurt? She examined the word covertly. Why should she feel hurt? Anger would be far more appropriate.

'Do you see much of Neville these days?'

The unexpected question caught her off guard and, remembering how she and Neville had treated him that summer, she coloured a little.

'Oh Neville's a regular visitor,' Fanny answered for her, giving her a teasing smile. 'Although she always denies it I suspect Lucy has a soft spot for him. Of course he's a very popular young man, more so since he's taken over his father's position in the business. Did you know about his connection with Holker's, the publishers? He was most helpful to Lucy with her book, wasn't he darling?'

Lucy felt her spirits plummet. It was all too easy to guess at the conclusions Saul had arrived at from Fanny's artless speech.

'It was my uncle who recommended Bennett's to me, not Neville,' she reminded her stepmother. 'We don't see quite so much of Neville as we once did.' she added, looking directly at Saul, 'but he does come down occasionally.'

He ignored her last statement to comment, with what she was sure was faked admiration, 'So you're writing a book. I'm most impressed Lucy. What's it about?'

As though he, too, had sensed the derision behind the surface pleasantry of the words, Oliver answered for her.

'It's all about the Martin family . . . And Lucy spends hours in the library reading all about them. It's going to be really good when it's finished.'

Fanny laughed indulgently. 'Really, Oliver darling. He quite dotes on Lucy,' she told Saul over the latter's head. 'Sometimes I feel quite jealous. But then of course the children have been spending so much time with her recently. And then of course, living here . . . in her house.'

There was a sudden silence while Lucy gazed incredulously at her stepmother. Did Fanny resent the fact that the Dower House had been left to her?

She frowned, shocked by the thought, swiftly banishing it. It was because Saul was here that she was having these unfair thoughts.

'Tell me more about this book of yours.'

Saul's question caught her off guard, a faint frown pleating her forehead as she looked at him.

'There isn't very much to tell really. I've finished the draft of the first book, and I'm due to go to London next week to discuss it with the publishers.'

'Mmm. What is it exactly? A history of the Martin family?'

'No . . . not really, although I have used family

papers and diaries as a background. It's a fiction work not a factual one, but by using the family documents I've been able to give it a strongly factual framework.'

He was looking at her in rather an odd way and rather belatedly Lucy realised that she had betrayed herself into her usual enthusiasm for her project. Instilling some of her earlier coldness into her voice she added, 'Of course, if you would rather that I don't use the library at the Manor from now on I shall understand.'

'Magnanimous of you.'

His dry tone made her flush as she realised how easily the cool voice she had used as a defence could be misconstrued as being rather haughty and supercilious.

She remembered now, too, how she and Neville had mocked his American accent, so different from their own British accents. How silly she had been to think it would be easy to wipe out the slights of the past. It was plain to her now that Saul felt nothing but contempt for her, and would doubtless laugh in her face if she were to attempt to apologise.

All in all she was extremely glad when he stood up and said that he had to leave.

'I have to go into Winchester to see the solicitors; apparently there's still a few loose ends to tie up.'

His smile when he left was for Fanny, not her, and it amazed her to realise how much that hurt.

CHAPTER THREE

FOR the rest of the week Lucy took care to avoid going anywhere near the main house and was rewarded by seeing nothing of Saul.

Tara had seen him, though, and the little girl appeared to have developed a rather unlikely case of hero-worship for him. George Martin had not been the sort of man to cherish his daughters and the feeling of desolation that bloomed inside her whenever Tara peppered her conversation with 'Saul said . . .' was an extremely disturbing one. Surely she couldn't be jealous? And if so, what of? The fact that Tara seemed to be transferring some of her dependence from her to Saul? Or the fact that Tara had found the solid male refuge a tiny part of herself had always secretly yearned for and been denied? It was impossible to give herself an answer.

Saul had been living at the house for five days when Fanny announced that she was spending the day in Winchester.

Lucy looked at her over her coffee cup. Both children had finished breakfast and were outside playing.

'Do you want to take my car?'

Fanny shook her head. 'No, it's all right. Saul's taking me.'

Slowly Lucy lowered her coffee cup, keeping her attention on it. As far as she was aware, Saul

had not been down to the Dower House since
that first visit, which must mean that Fanny had
gone to see him. But without mentioning it to
her?

Silly to feel hurt and yet she did. She and
Fanny had always got on well together despite
their very different temperaments, and never in a
thousand years could she imagine Fanny deliberately deceiving her.

'I wanted to talk to him about the children's
trusts.'

Numbly Lucy realised how defensive her
stepmother sounded.

'After all, Saul is the head of the family now,
Lucy.'

The head of the family? What on earth was
Fanny implying? Lucy knew how muddle-headed
she could be, but surely she could not possibly
believe that Saul owed them that sort of
responsibility?

'He was very kind and understanding,' Fanny
added. 'And he's taking me to see Mr Patterson,
so that he can explain everything to me.'

'But Fanny, he already has.'

Philip Patterson, the family solicitor, had
visited them on several occasions, just before and
then after George Martin's death to explain at
length the ramifications of his will and the trust
he had set up for Oliver and Tara.

'Yes, but he spoke to you, not me,' Fanny said
stubbornly.

Lucy frowned. 'But Fanny, you were there
with me . . .'

Across the table Fanny shrugged petulantly.

'Well yes. But I was so upset about your father. I couldn't take any of it in.'

There was a small silence while Lucy tried to assimilate her feeling of alienation and then Fanny said defiantly, 'I know you don't like Saul, Lucy, and that you resent him taking your father's place, but that doesn't mean the rest of us have to share your feelings.'

The unfairness of the criticism really hurt. So much so that for one awful moment she almost thought she might burst into tears. It was the unexpected direction from which the blow came rather than its weight, she told herself as she struggled to suppress the bleak desolation enveloping her. And Fanny was wrong; she did not dislike Saul.

'Luckily Saul's aware of how you feel about him. He told me he found you very anti when he came over that summer. I explained to him that it was quite natural really . . . what with you being aware that you couldn't inherit and that he would. It was bound to make you resent him.'

Lucy opened her mouth and closed it quickly, swallowing back the hot words of denial springing to her lips. She was angry, more angry than she could remember being for a long time. How dare Fanny make such careless assumptions about her feelings and actions, and even worse how dare she pass them on to Saul as though they were fact! It seemed to be a long time before she had control of herself sufficiently to say calmly,

'You're quite wrong, Fanny. I neither resent nor dislike Saul.' She wanted to explain to her stepmother her guilt over the past, but it was impossible to find the words, especially now when her anger still formed a hard lump in her throat.

An hour later, when Saul arrived, Lucy learned that the children were also included in the outing.

She didn't go downstairs, unable to trust her own reactions if she were to come face to face with him now. One thing was clear though. She could not allow this ridiculous belief that she resented him for inheriting the house to stand. When she felt calmer she would have to go and see him and explain the truth. She had been horrified by Fanny's careless revelation of what had been said, and the pride which had held her back from making an open apology for her foolishness all those years ago, when she realised he was not prepared to meet her equally openly, would have to be sacrificed to the truth. She was not going to allow him to go on thinking that she was stupid and small-minded enough to resent him owning the Manor.

From her own bedroom she heard the children racing about, doors slamming and then the expensive purr of Saul's car as he drove away.

Standing by her bedroom window, watching the car disappearing down the drive, she was once again swept by acute desolation. Could it possibly be a delayed reaction to her father's death? At the time she had been almost too busy to weep. And then there had been the shock of discovering that Oliver . . .

If anyone should resent Saul, it ought to be Oliver, but then in reality why should he? Her father had left Oliver more than well provided for, whereas Saul's inheritance was more of a burden than an asset.

The sunny morning had turned dull, and by lunch time it had started to rain. Lucy spent the afternoon in the comfortable sitting-room-cum-study which she had made her own terrain, sewing labels on to Oliver's new school clothes.

At half past four she heard the car, and although her body tensed, vibrating as though someone had touched a nerve, she made no move to get up.

The study door opened and she composed her face into a calm smile as she turned her head to the door.

But it was not Fanny and the children who came in, it was Saul. Her face felt as though it was caked in ice and about to crack, a violent tremor shuddering through her muscles.

Saul paused for a moment in the doorway, and her heart thudded as though suddenly struck a giant blow.

'I startled you. I'm sorry. Fanny asked me to call in on my way home to tell you that she and the children won't be back until after dinner. They ran into an old friend of your father's in Winchester, Colonel Bishop, and he invited them back to dine with him.'

'Thank you . . . I . . .'

Her tongue felt stiff, her lips unable to form the words. Thank God he had merely thought her startled. If he knew the truth . . . The truth? What was the truth? That something about this tall cool-eyed man touched her in a way so totally outside all her previous experience that part of her ached to repudiate him, even while another part longed desperately to be admitted to the most intimate circle of his life.

At twenty-five Lucy considered herself too old and too sensible for the folly of falling in love— that was an adolescent's game. So what was it that affected her so strongly about this man? Guilt alone did not explain away how she felt about him.

'Very domesticated.'

He was looking at the labels and the neat pile of garments she had already finished.

'For Oliver.' She was only half aware of what she was saying, too caught up in the need to absorb every minute detail of him, torn between a desire to prolong this moment of intimacy, and a frightened urge to end it.

'He starts his new school in September.'

'Yes.' He frowned. 'Your father's been extremely generous to his stepson, more so than to Tara or to you.'

'My father was rather old-fashioned. He held the view that boys need a good education and girls do not.' She risked a small smile at him and was relieved to see that he had stopped frowning.

'I owe you an apology.'

It was abruptly said, his face turning away from her so that she could read nothing in his eyes.

'I hadn't realised until today what a burden your father had put on you.'

Her heart leapt. Had Fanny told him about Oliver?'

His next words made it clear that she had not.

'Philip Patterson tells me that you're more or less wholly responsible for Oliver and Tara.'

'My father appointed me as their guardian along with Fanny,' Lucy agreed. 'I think he was worried that Fanny would not be able to cope alone—emotionally rather than financially.'

'So he burdened you with the responsibility for two young children plus your stepmother. Didn't either he or Fanny stop to think that you might want a life of your own? That you might marry . . . have your own children?'

'He did what he thought was best—for everyone,' Lucy told him quietly. 'Fanny . . .'

'Fanny is a clinging vine.'

He turned to look at her, and unbelievably he smiled.

The effect on her was dizzying . . . electrifying. She felt as though she were suspended in space . . . flying almost. She put down her sewing and stood up.

'Fanny told me this morning that she . . . that you possibly believe that I resent the fact that you have inherited the Manor.' She looked down at her own interlinked fingers, searching for the courage to go on. His smile had died and when she looked into his eyes they were not encouraging.

When he made no effort to help her she released her breath in a faintly helpless way and stumbled on. 'I want you to know that that isn't the case, Saul. I've always known that you would inherit and never resented it. In fact Neville probably . . .' She broke off, biting her lip, not wanting to use her other cousin as an excuse for her own behaviour. 'I feel your inheritance is probably more of a burden to you than an asset.' She looked directly at him now, forcing herself to meet and hold the cold grey of his eyes.

'I see . . . and it's because you don't resent me that you've been studiously avoiding me ever since I arrived, is that it?'

His voice was quite calm, but so underlined with cynicism that she was engulfed by despair. This was not how she had anticipated tendering her apology and explanation.

'Even Oliver and Tara seemed to think I was some sort of intruder . . . and they didn't get that from Fanny.'

'No, they got it from my father.'

The words were out before she could stop herself, and she bit down on her lip once again, angry with herself for being betrayed into that admission.

'OK, so you don't resent me. Fine.'

For some reason he seemed angry, thin lines carving cynically from his nose to his mouth. He turned, and she knew instinctively that he was about to go. Despairingly she reached out and touched his arm, and then withdrew in shock as she felt the warmth of his skin and the hardness of his bone beneath the covering of his casual shirt.

He looked at her, still frowning, watching her. Tension made her mouth dry, her tongue circling her lips defensively, watched by the narrowed gaze of those grey eyes. He was waiting, but she knew he would not wait for ever.

'Saul I owe you an apology as well.' She took a deep breath trying to steady her jumpy nerves.

He hadn't moved, but she was conscious of a difference in his stillness, a waiting quality that increased the tension already in the air.

'One that's over twelve years overdue,' she continued shakily. 'That summer when you came here I behaved appallingly, and I want you to know I've always regretted it. I hoped when you came this time we'd be able to make a fresh start . . .' She risked a faint grimace. 'Even that you might have forgotten how unkind I was. I'm afraid that summer was something of a traumatic one for me. I'd just lost my mother . . . and in those days I was too green to see through Neville. Not that I'm trying to shift the blame to him. I knew the way he was behaving was wrong. But I had a mammoth crush on him then and . . . Well, suffice it to say, since then I've learned exactly what he is—and isn't—and I've always regretted how I behaved; not because I knew you would inherit the Manor, I'd have regretted my behaviour whoever it was directed towards, but knowing that you, too, had endured emotional and family problems that year made it much worse.'

'Why didn't you say any of this to me when I arrived?' His voice was low and completely without any expression.

'I wanted to although I must admit I hoped it wouldn't be necessary. That you'd want to forget the past as much as I did and have a fresh start. Then when I realised you hadn't forgotten—or forgiven—I thought that if you had time to get to know me first my apology might have more worth . . . more reality.'

For a moment it seemed to her that he was simply going to turn away and leave her without a word and the pain that exploded inside her was almost unendurable, far more intense than something caused by a mere blow to the pride.

He turned away, lashes veiling his eyes, and she wondered what was going on inside his head, if he was weighing her words and finding them wanting; and then he was turning back to her, his mouth curling in a faint smile as he said easily,

'It was a bad summer for me. I knew my folks were on the point of divorce, and to be sent away to England, not knowing what my future might be and not able to do a single thing about it, made me angry. I guess both of us were operating under the same handicap and having Neville around didn't make things any easier.'

'No.'

Unsaid was the knowledge that without Neville's interference they might have found a way through their mutual distrust of one another, but Lucy was not going to tell him about her realisation of what her maternal cousin was right now.

'So I'm forgiven?'

The words trembled from her lips, her voice soft and unfamiliarly hesitant.

Saul smiled and leaned towards her, curling strong fingers round her wrists.

'When you look at me like that how can I say no?'

She hadn't completely lost all hold on reality, retaining enough sanity to say drily, 'Very easily I imagine, when I remember what a little beast I was.'

'Mmm . . . you certainly made it plain that you didn't want me around.' He laughed then, his eyes warming. 'It dealt quite a blow to my adolescent male pride to be so obviously cold-shouldered—something which Neville thoroughly enjoyed, as I remember.'

He saw her expression and his mouth curled in amused mockery. 'What's wrong? Didn't it ever occur to you that a boy of sixteen is quite capable of being hurt by the so obvious rejection of a girl of twelve?'

'I was only just twelve and you were almost seventeen,' Lucy reminded him huskily.

'And almost seventeen was quite definitely old enough to realise and appreciate the charms of a girl soon to be a woman.' He looked at her and laughed again. 'Didn't you realise later when you looked back how much of our mutual antagonism could be put down to mutual attraction, even if emotional rather than physical?'

Had she? Was that why Saul aroused such a powerful reaction in her now? With a small shock she realised he had said 'mutual attraction'. Did that mean . . .?

She looked at him and he said softly, 'Since we've now made our peace with one another we should perhaps seal it in the time honoured way.'

Almost as though he had known she would pull away from him and been prepared for it, his fingers tightened round her wrists refusing to let her go, and then with his eyes looking directly into hers he said lightly, 'Without the seal the peace treaty could be rendered null and void.'

And then he slowly uncurled his fingers from her wrists and let his hands hang free.

Without being aware of it she moved, swaying slightly towards him, taking that one step that would bring her close enough to his body to be aware of its strength and power. His eyes smiled into hers, teasingly, intoxicatingly, making her feel as giddy as an eighteen-year-old. And then his head bent towards her, his fingers sliding into the hair at her nape, gently angling her head so that her mouth was at exactly the right angle to meet his.

There was nothing forceful or demanding in the warm contact of his lips against her own; nothing at all in their almost fraternal pressure to make the world explode inside her in a blinding whirl of colours and sensations, but somehow it did.

As he kissed her she had automatically closed her eyes, but as he lifted his mouth from hers, the sensation of deprivation was so intense that her eyes flew open.

For what felt like a lifetime but was probably only a second he looked into them, and then both hands cupped her face, one thumb softly probing the moist fullness of her lips.

She responded instinctively, her head tilting back as she let him draw her even closer to his body so that she could feel the measured thud of his heartbeat against her skin.

Her eyes opened and watched the agonisingly slow descent of his head before her eyelids grew too heavy and fluttered closed. This time there was nothing fraternal in the touch of his mouth against her own.

Instinctively and willingly she met its demands, giving herself to the heady thrill of desire he aroused within her with a trust that would normally have appalled her. It was almost as though she possessed some instinct that overrode caution to tell her that with this man she would always be safe no matter what heights he urged her to scale.

When he released her she told herself she was not imagining it was with reluctance, and certainly there was a glitter in the darkness of his eyes that suggested he was as affected by their kiss as she was herself.

But now that he had set her free and her body was no longer being intoxicated by the heat of his, she reminded herself that she would be foolish to read too much into a mere kiss, and so as she stepped back from him she said as lightly as she could,

'Well then. Now we really are kissing cousins.'

The smile that curled his mouth made her pulses race. His eyes on her lips, he said softly, 'I certainly hope so.'

She was still half in a daze when the others came home. Oliver was full of the war stories the colonel had been telling him, and Tara was talking anxiously about the labrador puppies who needed a good home.

'Tom is such a sweet man,' Fanny told her when the children had been put to bed. 'And so thoughtful. He told me he thought I ought to get away for a little while ... have a holiday. Of course I told him it was out of the question. For one thing there simply isn't the money. And then I could hardly go off and leave you alone to cope with Oliver and Tara.'

At first inclined to agree with her, it occured to Lucy that her recent irritation with Fanny might have sprung from the fact that they were both still suffering the after-effects of her father's death and, that being the case, it might possibly be a good idea for Fanny to have a short break.

'If you wanted to go away I'm sure something could be arranged,' she suggested thoughtfully.

'Do you think so?' Immediately Fanny brightened. 'Tom did mention that a friend of his has an apartment in Marbella which he is sure I could rent for next to nothing.'

Privately Lucy doubted that, but she held her peace. They were not so short of money that Fanny couldn't go away if she wanted to and although she was determined to take a responsible and caring attitude towards her guardianship of the children, it was no part of her brief to monitor Fanny's spendings or say what she should spend her allowance on.

'I think it would do us both good,' Lucy told her generously. 'We're neither of us used to living so much on top of one another. The Dower House is quite sizeable compared with most houses, but it is an awful lot smaller than the Manor.'

'Oh, Lucy, you are a darling.'

She found she was being enthusiastically hugged. 'I'm sorry I've been such a beast lately. But I'm so lost without your father. Would you like me to speak to Saul and tell him that I was wrong—that you don't dislike him?'

Lucy shook her head, giving her a small smile.

'No—it's already done,' she told her wryly. 'By me!'

Within a couple of days everything was arranged. Fanny would fly out to Marbella at the weekend for a fortnight's stay in the colonel's friend's apartment.

During those two days Lucy had seen Saul on several occasions. Nothing personal had occurred between them, no reference had been made to the way he had kissed her or the way she had responded, but she was conscious of a complete change-about in his manner towards her and she basked in the warmth of it, like a small cat indulging herself in the heat of the sun after the coldness of winter.

Without her knowing it there was a subtle change within her, a certain feminine chemistry that made her more alluring ... softer. Tara noticed it.

'I really like living in the Dower House,' she confided in Saul one morning when he found her in the stables where he had insisted that Harriet remained.

'Lucy likes it, too. She's always laughing—and she cuddles me a lot. I like that!'

Lucy, coming into the stable in search of her just in time to catch her last words, felt herself go a vivid scarlet. Saul, who was looking at her, grinned as she turned to leave the stable; he paused beside her and murmured so that only she could hear, 'So would I!'

CHAPTER FOUR

FROM then on it seemed at though both she and Saul were possessed by an inner radar system that caused them both to gravitate to the same point at the same time.

Every time it happened Lucy found herself less and less sure that she was too old for the folly of falling in love. Saul only had to look at her and smile for her insides to start melting and her heartbeat to thud. And with every smile, every small gesture he made towards her, Saul said silently that her feelings were not hers alone. Outwardly there was nothing obviously lover-like in his behaviour towards her, but her senses so delicately attuned to his informed her that he was quite well aware of what it did to her when he placed his hand on her arm when he was talking to her, or pushed a wayward curl of hair back off her face with gentle fingers. And his eyes told her that he enjoyed the contact just as much as she did, promising that what was happening between them was merely a tentative, learning prelude to what was to be.

It pleased Lucy that he didn't rush her. Her feelings towards him were powerful enough to make her slightly afraid. Desire of such a voluptuous intensity was unfamiliar to her and, even while his touch delighted her, it was frightening to realise how vulnerable she was to him.

When they talked it was of commonplace, day-to-day things. She told him about Fanny's trip to Spain. He suggested that, since his car was the larger, he should transport Fanny to the airport, adding that if she cared to they could make a day of it, seeing Fanny off on her early morning flight and then going on to spend the day in London with Oliver and Tara. She responded gravely that she would put it to the children, already knowing they would not refuse.

Fanny was nervous on the Saturday morning of her flight, half inclined not to go, but by the time Saul pulled up outside she was feeling more cheerful.

In no time at all they were all in the car. Fanny and the children in the back, Lucy seated next to Saul in the front. Fanny had been about to take the front passenger seat but, by some dextrous manoeuvre, Saul had got her ensconced in the back. A tiny frond of pleasure uncurled inside her as Lucy sat beside him, content in the knowledge that he had wanted her there.

As they drove through the gates he slowed down and then stopped as their postman cycled towards them.

'You're getting an early start.' His smile encompassed them all as he handed two or three letters to Lucy and then reached past her to give a large bundle to Saul. Most of them seemed to have American stamps; business letters by the look of them, and it struck her how little she knew of the life Saul had lived in the States. Almost as though he knew what she was thinking he smiled at her before glancing wryly at his mail.

'From my company by the looks of it. I've taken some leave of absence to come over here, but it looks like some things won't wait.'

His words reminded Lucy that his stay in England could not be a permanent one. No doubt as soon as he had put the Manor on the market he would be returning to the States. An icy finger of dread touched her heart. What would happen to her then? If he were to ask her to go with him, would she?'

Her heart leaped at the thought. She would go anywhere with him, she acknowledged shakily, or at least she would had she been free to do so. She had her obligation to Oliver and Tara to consider . . . She shivered, forcing back a wave of desolation, and Saul, seeing it, looked at her with a concerned frown.

'Cold?'

She shook her head, retreating into silence as she tried to remind herself she had only known Saul a very short time; far too short surely to be thinking that, without him in it, her world would be a very desolate place indeed.

'Tired?'

Both children nodded sleepily in response to Saul's question as Lucy bundled them into the car.

After seeing Fanny safely off they had gone on to London, spending a few hours at the zoo before having lunch at a MacDonalds. A bus trip round the sights of the city, followed by afternoon tea at the Grosvenor House Hotel, and then a brisk walk through the park, had resulted in two very happy and very tired children.

'If we didn't have these two to think about, I'd suggest rounding off the day with dinner somewhere,' Saul told her as he drove home. Both children were fast asleep in the back of the car, and Lucy glanced back at them.

'Fanny's not exactly maternal is she?' Saul commented.

'In her own way she is.' Lucy felt bound to defend her stepmother. 'She loves them both very dearly.'

'But she's quite happy to let the responsibility for them rest on your shoulders.'

'I love them, too,' Lucy told him quietly, remembering how miserable she had felt earlier when she had contemplated the thought of him returning to America.

'I know you do. I suspect the man who marries you is going to find himself taking on the kids as well.'

Was he trying to find out if she would expect the children to live with her if she married? Up until today, she had never given much thought to her own future; marriage had seemed highly unlikely and certainly had been unwanted. But now . . .

'Not necessarily. Fanny is their mother and if I married I'm sure she would want them to live with her. The income she would get from her allowance and the trusts is enough for them all to live on, but of course I am their co-guardian and as such I would want to keep in touch with them.'

'Mmm ... Strange that ... After all, Oliver
has his own father doesn't he? I'd have thought
he'd be the one to support Oliver and not your
father.'

What on earth could she say? The knowledge
that she was actively deceiving him made her
tongue slow and her voice hesitant.

'My father loved Oliver very much.' It was
after all the truth. 'He was a man who much
preferred sons to daughters, and he and Fanny
married when Oliver was quite small.'

'Mmm ... Even so, it was rather odd, don't
you think, that he should make such generous
financial arrangements for a child who wasn't his
own?'

What could she say?

'He wasn't the sort of man whose decisions you
could question,' she told him, knowing that,
whilst her comment was the truth, it was only a
tiny part of it.

To get off such a potentially dangerous subject
she asked him curiously, 'What do you intend to
do about the Manor? Obviously you can't keep
it ...'

'No?'

It was more of a question than an agreement,
and she looked sharply at him.

'It would take a fortune to make it properly
habitable,' she reminded him, 'and even without
that, the rates and running costs alone ...'

'Mmm ... You're right of course. Don't you
feel any sentimental attachment to it at all, Lucy?'

Now it was his turn to be curious and this at
least was something she could answer honestly.

'Of course I do, but I'm afraid I'm also practical. During the last few months of my father's life, I had to take charge of running the estate, paying the bills and so forth, and I'm afraid that cured me of a lot of my sentimentality. Besides, I'd grown up knowing that one day I'd have to leave.'

'Yes, your father was very resentful of that entail, wasn't he? I remember that summer I came over, he never stopped reinforcing how much he disliked the thought of it coming to me. Was he very disappointed when Tara was born?' he asked her perceptively.

Lucy bowed her head so that he couldn't see her expression. 'A little,' she responded guardedly. 'Obviously you realised how he felt about the house—and the family. Up until the time my mother died I think I believed that somehow the Martins were immortal, inviolate, and way, way above the fate of other human beings. My mother's death taught me differently.

'So it wasn't resentment that summer—just pain.'

She liked him for seeing that.

'Yes,' she admitted.

'Well that's all behind us now.' He lifted his hand from the wheel briefly to cover hers, the contact warm and sure.

'I haven't seen you using the library since I've arrived. I hope that isn't because you don't think you're welcome?'

Initially it had been; that and a stubborn, difficult pride, but now . . .

She shook her head. 'I just haven't had time to

do any more work on my book. The draft of the first one is finished anyway and with the publishers. I'm going down to see them next week, and although I've been sifting through the diaries and letters for background information I don't intend to start on the second in the series until the first one's been passed and accepted.'

'You must be very good to have got this far,' Saul commented praisingly. 'I know how difficult it is for a new author to get a first book accepted, especially when it's fiction.'

'Well I was lucky in that my uncle was able to give me a recommendation,' Lucy reminded him modestly.

'True, but if your work hadn't been good enough, no amount of recommendations would have helped.'

Lucy knew that this was true, and it gave her a warm glow of pleasure to hear Saul's praise.

That was what she had missed since her mother's death, she acknowledged. Someone to share her ups and downs, no matter how small and trivial. Her father had never been interested in her writing, and Fanny, although kind-hearted, considered it a nonsense that any woman could actually want to work and become financially independent.

There was her uncle, of course, who she loved very much, but she didn't see that much of him, especially now that he had retired, and the fact that she and Neville no longer saw eye to eye tended to make her visits to his parents less frequent. Neville had his own flat in London, but Lucy always tended to feel a little uncomfortable in her aunt's presence, knowing how much she adored her only child. Her uncle, she suspected, saw his son more clearly, but he was a gentle, mild-mannered man, as far removed from his arrogant callous son as it was possible for a man to be.

'Will the books follow the fortunes of the Martin family?' Saul asked her, returning to the subject of her work.

'Very loosely. I'm going to use the more scandalous bits—the Martin who cost the family a title by refusing to go to bed with the Prince Regent will probably feature in it, and of course the family's trading connections, especially with the West Indies, make a very good background.

'Although I'm not up to that point yet, I'm thinking about incorporating the anti-slavery act, probably by using two brothers . . . twins maybe, one for and one against. I'd like to see the diaries and papers, if I may.'

'Wouldn't it have been easier for you to take them to the Dower House with you?'

'Yes it would, but they are family papers, and I felt they belonged to the Manor.'

'Rather a different view to your father's. I gather from my conversation with the solicitors that he managed to dispose of almost everything that might raise any cash.'

It was a just criticism and one she could not defend. She had privately considered it deplorable that her father should have stripped the house of its assets—assets that, had Saul inherited them, he would have been able to sell to keep the house going.

'I'm not my father, Saul.'

It was all she could say, and she knew from the warm touch of his hand against her own that he understood how she felt.

Although it wasn't very late when they got back, she felt tired enough to make her own way to bed less than an hour after she had tucked both children into theirs.

She and Saul had parted without so much as a kiss but she did not feel cheated or disappointed. The look in his eyes before he left her had told her there would be a time for them, and it had soothed her earlier fears about his imminent return to the States. Had he been questioning her about the children earlier because he did intend to ask her to go with him?

One step at a time, she told herself sleepily. One step at a time.

Her appointment with her publishers was fixed for Tuesday lunch time and on Monday Lucy went down to see the vicar's wife, to ask if she could possibly look after Oliver and Tara for the day. She had known Nancy Smallwood nearly all her life; Nancy's daughter Veronica was five years her senior and married now with two children.

'I'd love to have them,' Nancy assured her warmly. 'Veronica's bringing Daniel and Amanda down this afternoon—I'm looking after them for a week so that she and Ryan can have a break—so they'll be company for one another.'

'How's Saul settling in?' she asked, having met Saul the summer he had stayed at the Manor.

'Pretty well. Oliver was inclined to resent him a little at first, but now he tends to rather hero-worship him.'

'Oh well, that's no bad thing. A boy that age needs a man to model himself on. Does Saul intend to stay do you know?'

'I don't. I can't see how he would be able to keep the Manor on—that would take a fortune.'

'Yes. So what will he do—sell I suppose?'

'I expect so. He hasn't discussed it, but I don't see that he has much option. It won't be easy to find a buyer.'

'It would make a first-rate hotel—or a school . . . or even a convalescent home.'

She was right, and Lucy frowned slightly. The last time she had seen Neville he had been talking about a consortium he knew who might be interested in buying the Manor, but knowing Neville and his sharp practices Lucy doubted that any sale to Neville's friends would be very beneficial to Saul. She frowned harder, remembering how derogatory Neville had been about Saul the last time they met.

There had been an unpleasant degree of antipathy and contempt in his sneering comments about Saul's financial position and intelligence. She smiled rather grimly to herself. It might do Neville good to realise that Saul was not the hick country boy he seemed to think.

It didn't take her long to walk back from the vicarage. She had left the children in the care of Mrs Isaacs, and so she made her way up to the Manor without stopping at the Dower House.

When she got there there was no sign of Saul

and Mrs Isaacs told her that he had had to go out on business.

'Had a phone call from America he did this morning,' she confided expectantly to Lucy, but Lucy refused to be drawn, collecting the children and thanking her for looking after them.

Some last-minute doubts about her book kept Lucy at her typewriter until late afternoon. Her study was at the back of the Dower House so she wasn't aware that Saul had returned until Oliver burst in announcing, 'Saul's back. He's in the kitchen talking to Tara and he wants to see you.'

Pushing back her machine she got up, automatically flexing stiff muscles as she followed Oliver into the kitchen.

Saul was perched on the edge of the kitchen table, his back towards her as he bent his head in apparent engrossment towards Tara who was busily confiding to him her hopes that fat little Harriet might come away from the local gymkhana with a much prized rosette. As she walked in she was just in time to hear Saul agreeing gravely with Tara's views.

His head was turned towards the little girl, the strong tanned column of his neck exposed, the dark hair curling into his nape. Lucy had to subdue an aching impulse to reach out and touch him, to place her lips to that warm brown skin and breathe in the vital male scent of him.

Almost as though her thoughts reached out to touch him he turned, his eyes darkening as he read the message in hers before she could conceal it. A tide of guilty colour ran up under her skin.

She wasn't used to feeling such intense desire. Was Saul shocked by it? Amused?

A sense of uncertainty, of vulnerability, gripped her, leaving her feeling as embarrassed as a teenager held fast in the grips of an intense crush, and then Saul was smiling at her, his voice warm and vibrantly low, sending shivers of delight racing up and down her spine, as he said,

'I know you're away most of the day tomorrow, but I came to see if you'd have dinner with me in the evening. Tara tells me you've arranged for her and Oliver to stay at the vicarage.'

'Yes . . . I . . . Dinner would be lovely.'

He couldn't fail to be aware of her confusion, of the way he affected her, but there was no amusement or mockery in his eyes as he got off the table and came towards her, just a warmth that made her head suddenly feel extremely light and her legs oddly weak.

'What time do you leave in the morning?'

'Early,' she told him. 'I'm dropping the children off on my way.'

'Then I expect you'll want an early night tonight.' He smiled at her, warmly . . . intimately, she acknowledged, savouring that knowledge. If Tara and Oliver had not been there she thought he might have kissed her. Her heart started to thump unevenly, tiny *frissons* of excitement curling her nerve-endings.

'I like Saul, don't you?' Tara asked her later over supper. 'He's nice, isn't he?'

'Very nice,' Lucy agreed sedately while acknowledging to herself that 'nice' came nowhere near to describing Saul's personality.

As Saul had commented, she had intended to have an early night but although she went to bed, sleep eluded her, her mind not on the next day's interview, but on her dinner date with Saul.

Where would he take her? Somewhere quiet and secluded? A haunt of lovers? It seemed incredible that she, who had always been so cautious and withdrawn where men were concerned, should suddenly be so achingly eager for a man's desire. Even while part of her was faintly intimidated by the strength of her feelings for Saul, another part thrilled to the knowledge that she was woman enough to want him so intensely. Her lack of desire for her male escorts had never particularly worried her in the past—she had always been too busy to let it do so—but there was a tiny thrill of heady delight to be found in acknowledging how deeply Saul aroused her.

If she closed her eyes she could almost imagine the heat and pressure of his mouth on hers, his hands touching her flesh. The sensuous images that flashed across her closed eyes brought a slow ache to the pit of her stomach, activating a hitherto unsuspected vein of eroticism. Her tongue touched her suddenly dry lips, her nipples peaking urgently against the fine cotton of her nightdress.

Suddenly the night seemed far too warm, her body too keyed up for sleep. She wished it was tomorrow night and that she was with Saul . . .

Telling herself that such sexual urgency was undignified and foolish in a woman of twenty-five, she tried to control her disruptive thoughts and compose herself for sleep.

CHAPTER FIVE

THE heat in the centre of London struck her like a blow the moment she stepped out of the taxi. Her publishers had an office tucked away in a quiet and very exclusive mews, but the flowers in the smartly painted black and white tubs were rimmed with dust and looked tired.

She gave her name to the receptionist—a picture of glossy sophistication from her immaculately painted nails to her perfectly groomed hair. Once the sight of so much perfection would have automatically made her feel insecure, but now she could smile without envy at the other girl's city patina and even feel a little sorry for her because she was cooped up here in the heart of the hot city, and because she was not going home to have dinner with Saul.

She only had to wait ten minutes or so before going in to see her editor, and she passed the time glancing at the impressive-looking dust jackets displayed in the reception area. The publishers her uncle had referred her to handled fiction work in the main—they had several well-known names on their list; one of their writers was a well-known thriller writer, another a political correspondent turned faction author.

'Mrs Francis is ready to see you now.'

Dutifully Lucy followed the receptionist and was shown into a small office.

'Lucy, how are you my dear?'

Beverley Francis was only small, barely five foot two, her dark hair touched here and there with grey.

She and Lucy's uncle had been up at Oxford together, and she had the warm, but controlled, look of a woman secure in her position in life.

Shrewd brown eyes surveyed Lucy as she sat down.

'You look tired, and I'm not surprised. Your uncle was telling me the other day that things haven't been too easy for you since your father died.'

'Oh they haven't been too bad. There were one or two bumpy patches but we're over them now.'

'Umm ... You've got your stepmother and the children living with you I believe?'

Lucy's sensitive ears caught the faintly critical note skilfully hidden within the words, and automatically defended her father's actions.

'Fanny isn't really emotionally capable of handling things alone at the moment ...'

Looking at the finely-drawn features of the girl seated opposite her, Beverley Francis wondered a little at the thoughtlessness of a father who burdened a young woman with the welfare of his second wife and family. She had two stepchildren of her own—both married with families now—two girls whom she got on with very well indeed, but who by no stretch of her imagination could she see willingly taking on the role Lucy had been obliged to adopt.

'Look, I've booked our table for one o'clock,' she told Lucy, glancing at her watch. 'Shall we go straight there and discuss everything over lunch?'

When Lucy agreed, she got up, collecting her handbag and a small notebook.

The purpose of Lucy's visit wasn't mentioned again until they had been served with their main course, the conversation over their first course having been confined to Lucy's uncle and their days together at Oxford.

'We're really delighted with what you've done so far,' Beverley told Lucy without preamble, watching the tension ease out of her face. 'You do have a genuine natural flair for writing, Lucy. Of course there's a certain amount of smoothing out to be done, but nothing too drastic, and I can certainly tell you that we want to go ahead and publish. How much work have you done on the next book?'

'A lot of research, but very little else. I know what I'm going to put in it, and what main line the story will take, but I'm still mulling over the peripheral stuff—how much or how little I expand on the more remote family connections.'

Beverley listened closely whilst Lucy outlined her ideas for her second novel, interrupting occasionally to make a suggestion and to skilfully lead Lucy down by-lanes that hadn't previously occurred to her.

By the time they had finished their lunch, Lucy felt fired with a new enthusiasm to get back to her work. It had suffered during her father's illness and since then she had been too caught up with family affairs to give it the concentration it required—she had even begun to feel reluctant to go on at all. But now all that was banished and she was full of eagerness to get back to work.

When she said as much to Beverley, the latter laughed.

'That's what good editors are for—to inspire their writers, not depress them.'

They had talked over the minor points Beverley wanted to raise on her existing manuscript and when she eventually left the office midway through the afternoon, Lucy felt buoyed up and exultant. The re-writing work required was minimal—a smoothing off process rather than anything else, as Beverley had intimated, which she was confident she could have done within the time limit Beverley had set.

It was late afternoon before she got to the station, but luckily she didn't have long to wait for a train. As she got on to it she glanced rather guiltily at the glossy carrier over her arm. The silk suit she had seen in a Bond Street window had proved too much temptation to resist, the way the fabric clung to her body bringing vividly to mind her erotic imaginings of the night before. She would wear it tonight—for Saul.

The adrenalin which had pumped through her veins all afternoon increased its speed as the train slowed down for her station. She got out, her heart thudding furiously as she headed for her car.

'Lucy!'

Delight shocked through her as she recognised Saul's voice. He was striding towards her, almost grinning at her, his smile so wide while she stood like someone transfixed and waiting for him to reach her.

'I thought I'd come and pick you up—just in case you'd forgotten about our date.'

Forgotten? Her mouth curled into a smile at
the absurdity of the thought. She had her own car
parked only yards away and as she looked across
at it, she regained enough sanity to ask
breathlessly, 'But how did you know what train
I'd be on?'

Saul laughed, his voice faintly self-mocking as
he drawled, 'I didn't, so I've met each one.'

The curve of his mouth invited her to share his
amusement, but she couldn't. She was too
overwhelmed. Tears stung her eyes, her throat
closing up with a mixture of delight and anguish. It
had been years since anyone had cared enough
about her to do such a thing—in fact the last person
she could remember doing so was her mother.

'Hey . . .'

The bulk of Saul's body shielded her from
curious passers-by, his hand gentle and protective
as he turned her in towards himself, his eyes
concerned and faintly shadowed as he looked
down at her.

'I'm sorry . . .' What on earth must he think of
her? Shame scorched her face. Some explanation
was due to him, but what could she say apart
from the truth?

'You'll think me a fool I know, but it's just that
it's been so long since anyone cared enough for
me to do something as crazy as that.'

She thought she heard him swear softly under
his breath as his arms went round her, the solid
strength of his body supporting her as he drew
her against his warmth, her head seemed to fit
perfectly in the curve of his shoulder, her eyes
closing in blissful delight as she felt the light

movement of his lips against her forehead.

Abruptly he released her, his eyes glowing darkly.

'You're making it very hard for me to remember that I told myself I'd take things slowly,' he told her huskily.

'I'd better make my own way home—I can't leave my car here.' It was torture to step away from him, her senses brought achingly to life by the look in his eyes.

'Will an hour be long enough for you to get ready to go out?'

An hour? Being apart from him for more than five minutes would be sheer torture, but somehow she managed to nod her head and then walk away and get in her own car.

Later she decided it was a miracle she managed to drive home without incident. When she thought about it she could not remember a single thing about the drive, but she could remember how she had felt when Saul touched her, when he looked at her with that dark desire that made her blood pound and her pulses race.

As she stopped outside the Dower House he drove past her, sounding his horn and giving her a brief wave.

She collected her belongings and went inside. Suddenly an hour seemed far too short a time to get ready in. She was hot and sticky and in need of a shower. Her hair needed washing after the dustiness of the city. She had to ring the vicarage and check that all was well with the children.

She performed the last chore first, relieved to hear that all was going well.

'In fact I was going to ask you if they could stay another night, they're getting on so well with Amanda and Daniel.'

'Well if you're sure it's no trouble?'

'Not at all,' Nancy reassured Lucy. 'I'm enjoying it tremendously.'

They arranged that Lucy would pick them up on Thursday morning.

As she replaced the receiver Lucy realised with a tiny kick of pleasure that she would have a second night of freedom . . . a second night when . . . When what?

Betrayingly her body remembered the hard warmth of Saul's against it, and putting shaking hands against her hot cheeks Lucy warned herself not to get too carried away.

The vibrant fuchsia pink of her outfit, so hard for someone with the paler eyes normally associated with her colouring to wear, looked stunning against the foil of her darker skin and richly warm eyes.

The summer had given her a good tan, at the same time highlighting her blonde hair, and the effect of the vivid silk against her warm brown flesh and Nordic pale hair had a visual impact that even she found faintly startling.

It was warm enough for her to go bare legged, a pair of high-heeled sandals emphasising the slender delicacy of her ankles.

At twenty she had been faintly podgy, but that puppy fat had soon disappeared, and in the anxiety of her father's illness and subsequent death she had lost more weight—perhaps just a shade too much, she thought judiciously, studying the narrow flatness of her hips, and wondering anxiously if Saul would find such slenderness unfeminine.

She kept her make-up to a minimum, just the merest dusting of highlight across her cheekbones, its pinky tones echoed in her lipstick and eyeshadow. Perfume was something she rarely wore—her lifestyle made it unsuitable; she found it cloying during the daytime, and went out so rarely at night that she never bought any, but this evening she had filched some of Fanny's bath oil—a perfume she did not recognise, *Lutèce*, but which now enveloped her in a delicately scented cloud.

Saul was five minutes early, for which he apologised as she opened the door to him. It was a new sensation for her to have someone so eager for her company, so much so that part of her cautioned her against getting carried away, warning her that the emotion and desire she could read in Saul's eyes could be as ephemeral as a daydream.

But there was nothing ephemeral about the way he smiled at her as he studied the lissom slenderness of her body before helping her into the car; nothing ephemeral about the touch of his fingers against her skin as he brushed against her arm when fastening her seatbelt.

His touch brought out a rash of goosebumps, the tiny hairs on her arm standing on end as she shook with a delicate shudder. She saw his eyes darken and his body tense as it responded to the signals of her own and felt desire flower inside her as she realised that he shared her need.

He had booked a table at a restaurant several miles away in a peaceful riverside setting.

Lucy knew it by repute but had never dined there before, and because it was only early in the week the dining-room was only pleasantly full.

When they didn't have drinks in the bar but went straight to their table, Lucy thought that Saul must be hungry, but as she was studying the menu an ice bucket and champagne arrived.

'As far as your book's concerned, I don't know yet whether this will be to celebrate or commiserate,' he told her softly as the waiter filled their glasses with the foaming liquid. 'But I certainly want to celebrate my good fortune in being here with you tonight, Lucy.'

The champagne slid coolly down her throat, fizzing intoxicatingly, the texture deliciously dry.

They drank to one another, and then to Lucy's book, when she told him how well her meeting had gone.

She ordered melon sorbet to start with, followed by salmon, ridiculously delighted when Saul chose the same. It seemed a good omen that their tastes should be so much in accord.

Knowing the reputation of the restaurant Lucy was sure the meal was a poem of epicurean delight, but she barely registered it; she was too absorbed in Saul, in listening to him, in just simply watching him.

He caught her doing so once, their eyes meeting, locking in a way she thought belonged only to the world of films. Her heart seemed to stop completely, and then bound into ecstatic life as Saul reached across the table to curl his fingers round her own.

'I can't believe this is happening.'

His words echoed her own thoughts and she grimaced faintly. 'I know ... It seems faintly ridiculous.'

'Ridiculous?' He looked at her and then shook his head. 'No. Miraculous, maybe ... but ridiculous—never. I've waited a long time to feel this way about someone, Lucy, and now that I do I want to savour every moment of it ... every second ... We won't rush things, grabbing greedily at sexual fulfilment before we've tasted all the delicate ancillary pleasures of courtship. I'm twenty-nine years old and I want more from this relationship than sex.'

'More?' Her voice sounded husky and unsure. What was he trying to say to her? 'What sort of more?'

She watched him smile, knowing with an involuntary ache that no matter how long her life might be she would never forget the way he smiled.

'Oh, commitment ... permanence ... That sort of more.' He said it teasingly, but his eyes were serious. Her heart jolted and lurched within her.

'I'm rushing you—something I promised I wouldn't do. I don't want to frighten you off. Let's talk about your book.'

'I want to talk about you,' Lucy wanted to protest, but she felt too weak to argue, to do anything other than follow his lead. Was this love? This heady, almost delirious feeling that possessed her; this ridiculous happiness that invaded her simply because they were together?

It was late when they left the restaurant. Because he was driving Saul had insisted that Lucy finished off the champagne, and on top of the wine they had had with their meal and the brandy after it, it had made her feel faintly tipsy.

Sauls' hand closed over hers as they walked to the car, his arms coming round her as they stopped beside it, his mouth warm as it feathered softly on hers.

The urge to cling to him and go on clinging almost overwhelmed her and she had to fight to remind herself that they were standing in a public car park, and to step away from him as his mouth completed its languorous exploration of hers.

'Very wise,' he teased softly, letting her go. 'Otherwise I might have forgotten all my good intentions.'

'Maybe that's what I'd like you to do— somewhere more private.' She could hardly believe the provocatively husky words had come from her tongue, but they had, and judging by Saul's arrested expression and glinting eyes, he was nowhere near as shocked by them as she was herself. Quite the contrary.

'One day, not very far from now, I'm going to remind you of those words,' he promised her, releasing her to unlock the car door.

They were more than halfway back before the heated excitement had faded from her blood. She wanted him quite desperately, she recognised, to the extent that if he took her home with him now, she would willingly go with him.

The Dower House was reached all too quickly.

Neither of them had spoken since getting in the car, but words had been completely unnecessary. As Saul brought the car to a halt, Lucy hesitated.

'Do I get invited in for a nightcap?'

Her eyes flew to his face. Had he guessed how reluctant she was for the evening to end? As she met the look he turned on her face she knew that he had.

There was something subtly exciting about knowing that beneath the surface conventionality of the trite remark ran a deep and dangerously powerful current of desire, something exhilarating and faintly wicked in playing this game, to respond casually to his teasing comment and invite him in, as though almost bored by his suggestion.

The house was in darkness and as he followed her into the hall while she fumbled for the light switch she was intensely aware of him standing behind her. Her fingers reached for the switch, her mind tormenting her with vivid mental images of Saul reaching out towards her, turning her, enfolding her in his arms.

'Having trouble?'

The calm casualness of his question was shatteringly down to earth. As his hand reached unerringly for the switch, by-passing hers to do so, she wondered if she was suffering from some sort of self-delusion. There was nothing remotely lover-like in his voice now, or in the way he was looking at her.

At least there hadn't been. She tried to swallow as she saw the look in his eyes and found that she couldn't.

'Lucy . . .'

Her name was a tormented cry of wanting breathed against her lips, his mouth smothering any verbal response she might have made. One of them was shaking violently—or was it both of them?—the hot urgency of their kiss overwhelmingly intimate. It got harder and harder for her to breathe, but to tear her mouth from Saul's was to die. Her body leaned on the strength of his, warmed and supported by it, frustrated by the barrier of their clothes. His mouth released hers, his tongue tip touching her full lips.

'Coming inside with you was an idiotic idea,' Saul whispered against her mouth. 'I should have known what would happen.'

His words made her go cold with rejection.

'You were the one who . . .'

'I know . . . I know . . .' The softness of his voice soothed her defensive protest. 'I want you like hell, Lucy,' he told her rawly, 'And I know damn well that when I leave here I'll spend the rest of the night lying awake wishing you were with me, but we've got to take it slowly before we become completely blinded by physical desire. I want to know you as a person as well as a woman. Does that make any sense to you?'

It made beautiful sense, humbling and disconcerting her, making her throat close up on a wave of emotional vulnerability.

'I want more from you than sex,' he added huskily, 'Much, much more.'

He leaned forward, his mouth gently brushing first her eyes and then her mouth, and then he released her. Her eyes opened reluctantly.

'Now, how about that nightcap, and while we're drinking it we can reminisce about old times, and then, when I have drunk the cup of coffee you're going to make me, I shall get up and say good night and go home to my lonely bed!'

And that's the way it was. And later on, sleepless and too wound up emotionally and physically to care, Lucy was torn between the happiness of knowing that Saul wanted more for them than a relationship based only on sex, and an aching disappointment that his self-control was so resolute—far more resolute than her own, she acknowledged, feeling the heat beat up through her body once more as she re-lived his good-night kiss.

There had been a moment then when she had sensed that it would take very little to push him over the edge, to incite him to abandon caution.

His hand had touched her breast, unerringly finding its taut peak, and she had sighed her pleasure against his mouth, feeling in the fierce clench of his muscles and the slow, reluctant way he drew away from her, how difficult it was for him.

If she had refused to let him go they would have been lovers by now, but Saul was right; their relationship, their feelings and trust of one another were too new for them to plunge into the heady waters of passion together yet. Tonight they would be alone again.

She fell asleep on that thought, clutching it to her while her features curved into an expression of anticipatory bliss.

*   *   *

Following her discussions with her editor, Lucy had decided to make use of her unexpected day of freedom from looking after the children working on her second novel.

After a skimpy breakfast of coffee and toast, all she could manage in her present highly emotional state, she collected her notebooks and portable typewriter and made her way to the main house.

Mrs Isaacs greeted her cheerfully as she went in the back way. 'Mr Saul told me to expect you,' she announced. 'Said you would be working in the library, but that I was to make sure I dragged you away for some lunch. He's had to go out himself, but he said to tell you he'd be back at twelve.'

Saul seemed to be doing a fair amount of 'going out' at the moment. On business connected with the house perhaps? As yet they had not talked about the Manor and Saul's plans for it—they had been far too busy talking about more important things. He would have to sell it, of course, and finding a buyer might be difficult. The thought of the house going out of the family did cause her a faint pang, but it was only faint. Houses as large and old as this one was were too much of a burden for anyone less than a multimillionaire to own and run. However, no doubt Saul would be anxious to settle his affairs and get back home to his job.

Ridiculously they hadn't even discussed what he did for a living. A small smile touched her mouth. Whatever it was it was scarcely important as long as it made him happy. Everything he had said to her implied that when he did return to

America he would ask her to go with him, and she knew that she would have some hard thinking ahead of her if he did. She had a responsibility to Oliver and Tara from which she could not wholly abdicate, but she was no suffering martyr and had no intentions of sacrificing her own happiness to assume the duties which should by rights be Fanny's.

No, something could be worked out. It would have to be, she decided grimly, her full lips tightening briefly as she dwelt on the scenes that were likely to occur with her emotional step-mother. It didn't matter what scenes Fanny caused; her love for Saul came first.

Love! The taste of the word made her go dizzy with pleasure. Her feelings for Saul had trans-formed her from a level-headed young woman into a starry-eyed child, full of wonderment and joy. Her hitherto sedate view of what happiness was had been totally overthrown. It was like discovering that the rare, shimmering mirage was real after all and moreover could be reached out to and touched.

Reluctantly she dragged her mind away from Saul and on to her work, and yet, as she concentrated on the outline for her second book, with maddening insistence her central male character kept appearing to her as Saul.

In the end she gave in to her desire to paint a verbal portrait of him, knowing when she had finished and read through what she had just written that she had breathed so much life into the character that no one could ever believe he was simply a work of fiction.

True to his promise Saul was back for twelve and she was out of her seat and halfway towards the library door the moment she heard his footsteps outside.

The phone rang while he was kissing her and he disengaged reluctantly, holding her within the curve of his arm as he picked up the receiver.

As she watched his mouth grew taut, his eyebrows drawing together in a faint frown.

'OK Ma, I get the picture,' he said abruptly at last. 'But it's impossible for me to get back right now.'

He was silent again, listening to whatever it was his mother had to say. His mother! Lucy had never met her father's sister. Were they alike at all? What would she think of Saul's involvement with her? Was she one of those impressively organised American matriachs who already had a suitable partner picked out for her son?

'No, I don't know how long I'll be—as long as it takes.' He listened again briefly, and then replaced the receiver.

'Problems?' Lucy asked him worriedly.

Her weight was supported against his body and she liked that, liked the feeling of permanence and safety that emanated from him. He felt as steady as a rock—and as hard. The thought briefly made her feel cold. Saul would be a dangerous man to cross, she recognised, seeing in the way he was frowning the irritation of a man used to making his own decisions about his life, without having them queried or crossed.

'A hiccup in my stepfather's business affairs and

my mother wants me to return home to sort them out.'

He saw her faint frown and explained, 'I work for him.'

That explained how he was able to take so much time off, Lucy realised, wondering again what it was that he did.

'I'm an accountant—of sorts,' he added curtly, and she realised that his work was not something he wanted to discuss.

'Will you have to go back?'

'Not right away.'

The tension in the muscles of his arm where it lay against her body comforted and yet alarmed her. He didn't want to upset her by saying he might have to go, but she sensed that it was quite possible.

It was still too soon for him to ask her to go with him—at least as his lover—and she prayed feverishly that whatever the problem was at home, it would be solved without the necessity of him having to rush back.

'Are you any closer to finding a buyer for this place?' she asked him, trying to change the subject. Disposing of the Manor must be a burden to him when he obviously had so many responsibilities at home.

'There are one or two possibilities,' he told her cautiously, 'but one always has to be aware as a foreigner that the locals might be trying to gain an advantage. How do you really feel losing this place, Lucy?' he asked her abruptly. 'You must feel some attachment to it.'

'Yes, but probably only in the way that you

do,' she agreed mildly. 'After all it isn't as though it really belongs . . .' She broke off, appalled by her near indiscretion. How close she had been then to blurting out the secret of Oliver's birth. She risked a look into Saul's face, anticipating his curiosity, but instead his expression was curiously blank, his arm instantly slackening to release her.

As he turned away from her he said evenly, 'How delightfully British you are at times, Lucy. I see that you do after all consider me something of an interloper here.'

She was horrified by the way he had misinterpreted her words. 'No . . . no, Saul,' she appealed to him. 'You're quite wrong. I don't see you as an interloper at all.'

'But neither do you see me as the rightful owner here, is that it?'

What could she say? Legally he was the rightful owner, but she knew he did not have the soul-deep feeling for the place that her father had had and which he had passed on to Oliver, in whom she sensed the same emotion, young though he was. But how could she break the promise she had made to her father and tell Saul this? And what good would it do anyway? Saul might even think she was trying to manipulate him into doing something for Oliver.

When she was silent he laughed shortly, turning round to glare at her as he said harshly, 'What a pity you didn't fulfil your father's hopes for you, Lucy, and marry money.' He saw her expression and jeered softly. 'Oh come on, surely you aren't going to tell me you don't know? Even my mother knew, although she flatly refused to help him when he asked her to launch you on the American season and introduce you to a few potential millionaires. The days are gone when they were willing to part with their money in exchange for an aristocratic wife. No doubt he was hoping that your wealthy husband would buy this place from me after his demise, thus securing it for his grandchildren.'

Lucy was completely stunned by what he was saying. He was making it up, he must be; her father had never once said a word of this to her.

'You think I'm lying don't you?' Saul demanded almost savagely. 'Well I'm not—ask my mother. I think you were about seventeen when your father made his first approach.'

Seventeen! Lucy thought back weakly. Fanny had still been married then. And who knew? Perhaps her father, who had always had a penchant for crazy schemes, had dreamed up something along the lines Saul was suggesting.

'I don't think you're lying Saul.' She said it quietly so that he wouldn't mistake the conviction in her voice. 'It sounds just like the sort of thing my father would do. If I seemed disbelieving it was because he never mentioned any of this to me. I know he hoped Fanny would give him a son; and as you say he was almost obsessed with the idea of keeping the house for his own heirs.'

'Almost?' Saul derided bitterly.

'Very well then, totally.'

A certain bleakness shadowed her eyes as she remembered how she had suffered from her father's obsession. A sensitive child, it had not taken her long to recognise that she was not the child he had wanted—not a son.

As though he knew her thoughts Saul gave a kind of groan and came towards her, taking her in his arms, holding her fiercely.

'Forgive me. I had no right to say any of those things to you. The plain fact is that I'm jealous—jealous of the loyalty you give your father—and half scared to death that I'll have to go home before I can persuade you to come with me.'

His admission soothed away the hurt. She turned her face up eagerly, her lips parting in soft invitation.

It was a long time before he released her, his voice faintly shaky as he asked, 'Do I take it that that means that you would come?'

'Anywhere—with you,' Lucy told him, sighing the words against his throat, her eyes closing in bliss as she tasted the masculine flavour of him. It was true. She would follow him to the ends of the earth if he asked it of her. It was too late for pretence now. She was deeply, crazily in love with him—he was the only thing that mattered and if he left her now she thought she might go crazy with the agony of losing him. It was a novel sensation for her, and one that would once have terrified her, but which she now revelled in, knowing that she wasn't alone, that he shared her feelings.

Over lunch he told her a little more about his stepfather, explaining that he was in his seventies and in rather poor health. 'My mother adores him, although you'd never realise it. He has two daughters from his first marriage and five grandchildren; my mother's always complaining that it's time I produced some, too.'

'And your father,' Lucy pressed. Do you see much of him?'

'A little. He lives in Boston now. He married the daughter of a newspaper magnate and he has a second family. Everything's very amicable but in many ways I feel closer to Harry. After all, he was the one who was there during the time I was growing up. He paid for me to go to college and later on to qualify as an accountant—housed and fed me, gave me a job. In fact he was far more of a father to me than my own ever was—and made a better job of it, I suspect, when I see my two half-brothers. My father's a workaholic. Always was and always will be. That's what led to my parents' divorce in the first place.'

He went on to tell her about the old winery his parents had bought in California and the lifestyle they lived there, and when he excused himself after lunch, explaining that there were some phone calls he had to make, if only to set his mother's mind at rest, Lucy made her way back to the library feeling that she now knew far more about him.

At two o'clock he put his head round the door and announced that he had some papers he wanted to catch the post and that he intended to drive into Winchester to make sure they did.

'Mrs Isaacs is leaving us something cold for supper and I'll bring some steaks back with me,' he told her, coming into the room to draw her up into his arms and kiss her thoroughly.

'You know,' he muttered seconds later, sensually nuzzling the tender skin of her throat, 'in view of the developments at home, I'm beginning to wonder if a long, slow courtship's such a good idea after all ... particularly when there's nothing, but nothing, I'd like more right now that to take you to bed.'

She couldn't control the quiver that ran through her and knew when he laughed softly that he had felt it, too, and knew its origins.

'Very flattering,' he whispered, his breath tickling her ear. 'I'm almost tempted not to bother with the post.'

'Mrs Isaacs is still here,' Lucy pointed out demurely, but her eyes were a deep sparkling brown, her skin flushed with colour, her body melting, eager for all that he was promising.

'Later,' he growled mock-threateningly as he released her. 'Later I'll make you sorry for that—when she isn't here to protect you.'

They kissed again lingeringly and then he was gone, leaving her to pick up the remnants of her shattered control and try to work.

At three o'clock, long before she had expected Saul back, Lucy heard a car.

Curiosity drove her from her chair to the window, her mouth compressing slightly as she saw Neville extricating himself from the driver's seat of his sports car.

At thirty-one his face showed the manner of man he had become: greedy, grasping and selfish in the way that only the weak could be. Lucy knew that her uncle was bitterly disappointed in his son. Not so much in the way he ran the business—Neville was an astute businessman although his methods weren't those of his father; no, it was his inner moral code—or lack of it—

that most hurt her uncle. Sometimes Lucy felt
that Neville almost enjoyed hurting others.

He smiled as he saw her, the calculating
ingratiating smile that told her he must want
something. Neville had wanted many somethings
from her over the years, but now she was immune
to the shallow charm he turned on so effortlessly,
tolerating him only for the sake of her uncle.

He came in via the drawing-room french
window and would have embraced her if Lucy
hadn't adroitly avoided him.

'Our colonial cousin nowhere in evidence I
see?'

The sarcastic twist to his lips as he referred to
Saul infuriated Lucy but caution urged her to
hold her tongue. Neville had always been
remarkably clever about recognising weakness in
others and then turning it to his own advantage.

'Have you come down to see him?' She kept
her voice carefully neutral, noting that Neville
had left the french windows open.

'Sort of. But I wanted to have a chat with you
first.'

Again that winning smile. Once she had made
the mistake of aligning herself with Neville
against Saul, and she would never totally forgive
herself for that mistake, but she was careful not
to allow any of her distaste to show in her face,
saying lightly instead, 'I'm flattered.'

'Oh no you're not,' Neville told her softly.
'You hate my guts.' He smiled coldly at her
stunned expression. 'Whatever else you might be
you're no actress, cos, but you do owe me a
favour and I'm calling it in.'

'A favour?'

'The recommendation to Bennett's that they read your manuscript,' he reminded her mockingly. 'Surely you don't think anyone would have paid it a blind bit of notice otherwise?'

What was he implying? Lucy looked at him suspiciously.

'OK, I'm sure the book's well enough written, but well written books are a hundred a penny—you know that. Without my father's pull, it would never have got past the first read—if it had made it that far.'

There was enough truth in his statement to make her hesitate to deny it. There were hundreds of other writers far more skilled than she was herself—she knew that, but she had been lucky enough to have an entrée into the publishing world. Even so . . .

'What sort of favour Neville?' she demanded sharply.

'Nothing too painful,' he assured her, giving a soft, satisfied laugh as she capitulated. 'Some business friends of mine are interested in buying this place—at the right price of course.' He saw her expression and laughed softly, 'Oh come on, Lucy, don't give me that look. All I want you to do is to drop a word in old Patterson's ear that you've heard of someone who's interested in buying the place. He thinks a lot of you—he's always had a soft spot for you. As far as we know no one else is interested in buying.'

'So why go about making your offer in such an underhand way?' Lucy asked hotly. 'Why not approach Saul openly and honestly?'

Neville laughed jeeringly. 'Oh come on—you know the answer to that. He'd never sell this place to us if he knew I was involved.

Lucy knew that Neville spoke the truth. On the surface his request seemed perfectly feasible . . . and yet . . . 'What is it exactly you want me to do?' she asked him suspiciously.

'I just want you to have a word with old Patterson and find out if anyone else is interested and if so . . .'

'You said they weren't,' Lucy reminded him sharply, watching him shift uncomfortably from one foot to the other. She didn't trust Neville; his request, on the surface so reasonable, seemed to her to be just an excuse, a front to hide his real purpose behind, but unless she played along with him a little she would have absolutely no chance of discovering what that purpose was. And she wanted to find out because instinctively she knew it threatened Saul.

'Come on Lucy, you owe me a favour.'

Normally she would have reminded him that it had been his father who had helped her to find a publisher, but now she kept silent, pretending to consider for a few seconds.

'Well?'

'I'll do what I can,' she fibbed, smiling at him, 'but first of all I want to know exactly what's going on.'

He looked so satisfied that Lucy knew she had been right to distrust him. Alarm leapt along her veins as she contemplated his gloating expression.

'Well . . . why not,' he agreed grinning at her. 'After all, you've got about as much love for our wild colonial usurper as I have myself, haven't you?

'There's a whisper in the City that the Government are planning to build a new armaments place down here. I picked it up in my club from an old school chum. They haven't fixed on a site as yet, but it's odds on that it will be within a couple of miles or so of this place. There's a lot of money going into it, and lots of top brass involved.

'All those people stuck down here are going to want somewhere to let off steam and enjoy themselves, and that's where this place comes in. If we could get it at the right price, we can turn it into a hotel-cum-sports complex to outclass any in the country. We'd make a real killing, especially if we can buy it off little ol' Saul for peanuts. And that's where you come in, my love. A word from you to Patterson will almost guarantee that we can get the place at a knock-down price, especially if you told him that you were involved as a shareholder—which you could be. If I know my uncle's solicitor he'll be thinking that you're getting a pretty raw deal out of the estate.'

His words came very close to the truth, her father's solicitor had never approved of what her father had done and had said so. He was also very fond of her and would no doubt be prepared to look favourably on a request from her, but she felt sure that Neville misjudged him when he hinted that he might put her interests before Saul's. The solicitor was far too honourable and honest for that, but she was not going to tell Neville that.

What frightened her most was the knowledge that, if there were no other buyers, Saul could well be forced to part with the house at a knock-down price to Neville and his business friends, leaving them to make a good deal of money out of their acquisition.

'Well, Lucy, what do you say?' His voice had dropped caressingly as he came to stand beside her, both of them framed in the light from the french window as he pulled her into his arms. Lucy had to fight against flinching away from him, praying that he wouldn't guess at her real feelings. For Saul's sake she mustn't betray to Neville what she was feeling, at least until she had had the chance to tell Saul what he planned. Who knew, she thought feverishly, her mind chasing round in frantic circles, perhaps, with his stepfather's business acquaintances, he might be able to raise enough money for such a conversion himself?

'For old time's sake? Remember what a fool we made of him that summer? Wouldn't you enjoy doing it all over again?'

Urging herself to play for time, Lucy swallowed her loathing of all that her cousin was suggesting and said huskily, 'Perhaps.'

'Of course you would. This place should have been yours, not his. You'll use your charm to get round him then?' he asked, referring once more to the solicitor. 'It shouldn't be too hard.'

'I'll do my best.' Her voice sounded breathless, strangled by her dislike of what she was doing and her panic that Neville might guess that she was lying.

'You'd better leave,' she cautioned him. 'Saul will be back soon.'

He frowned and then nodded his head.

'Perhaps you're right. How long do you think it will take you to bring him round? A couple of days?'

Him? Once again Lucy realised Neville was talking about the solicitor. 'I'm not sure. I'll give you a ring.'

'Umm. I'll give you a ring the day after tomorrow to see what progress you've made.'

She had to force herself to stand still when he kissed her, loathing the feel of his mouth against her own. But at last she was free, her mind and stomach both churning hopelessly as she watched Neville disappear through the french window. Seconds later she heard the roar of his car engine fade into the thick silence.

Dear God, she hoped that Saul would be back soon. There was so much she had to tell him. She couldn't work, not now, so instead she went back to the Dower House intending to shower and change for the evening.

CHAPTER SIX

SHE heard Saul's car as she was putting on her make-up, her fears forgotten as she flew to her bedroom window in time to see it disappearing up the drive.

Disappointment ached through her that he had not thought to stop, but then, she reasoned to herself, he was not likely to realise she was here. She glanced at her watch. Almost half past six, not too early surely for her to turn up for their dinner date?

She decided to walk to the house, and passed Mrs Isaacs on the drive as the other woman was on her way home. She slowed down her car and leaned out of the window to say worriedly to Lucy,

'There's something worrying Mr Saul. Came in in a real strange mood he did, and now he's in the library drinking whisky.'

Worry etched a small frown line on her forehead as Lucy hurried up to the house; even allowing for a degree of embellishment Mrs Isaacs voice had held enough genuine anxiety to make her wonder what had happened. Had Saul received another telephone call from America? Was his stepfather's health showing more signs for concern?

She called out to him as she entered the hall and receiving no reply hurried into the library.

The moment she saw his face all her worries about Neville and his plans left her. Saul was frowning, nursing a glass of whisky, as he turned to look at her broodingly.

'Saul what on earth's wrong? Is it your stepfather? Is something wrong at home?'

As she flew towards him, it seemed for a second or so that he almost flinched back from her, but no, she must have been mistaken because his fingers were now curling round her upper arm, almost painfully tightly she realised, but such was her concern for him that she didn't bother to draw this to his attention.

He was looking at her in a very odd way, she realised, searching her face, almost desperately.

'Saul ... What is it?' She reached out pleadingly towards him, smelling the spirit on his breath. 'Something's happened, hasn't it?' she demanded positively.

His mouth curled into a totally humourless smile, his expression one of such frozen bleakness that it made her shiver. She had never seen such a cold look in anyone's eyes before.

'You could say that, but now isn't the time to talk about it!' He was abrupt with her almost to the point of dislike.

'Would you prefer me not to stay?'

She had to ask him the question, barely recognising the man who had been so tender towards her in this cold, almost frightening stranger.

'No ... No, stay.' He turned away from her, pouring himself another drink, she noticed worriedly, his back to her as he asked tonelessly,

'Did you get much done this afternoon?'

'Er . . .' Now was her chance to tell him about Neville, but how could she add to whatever was already on his mind?

'So . . . so.'

'I went to see Patterson this afternoon,' he told her abruptly. 'He advises me to sell this place. What do you think?'

His question caught her off guard, and without thinking she replied absently, 'I don't see that you've much option. It would cost a fortune to live in.'

'Your father managed it,' he reminded her tersely.

Lucy didn't need reminding that what few assets the estate had possessed which might have benefited it had been realised by her father for Oliver's benefit. A faint tinge of guilty colour washed her skin at Saul's bitter tone.

'By the skin of his teeth,' she agreed quietly.

'So you think I *should* sell then?' he asked her curtly.

He was looking at her now, his eyes glittering almost feverishly, high colour burning over his cheekbones almost as though he had a fever. He looked ill, Lucy realised worriedly, his skin beneath that hectic flush an unhealthy greyish colour.

'Saul. What is it?' She went towards him automatically, stopping in shock when he raised his hands as though to rebuff her.

'You haven't answered my question yet, Lucy,' he told her harshly. 'Would you advise me to sell—to get rid of this place as quickly as

I can before it becomes a millstone round my neck?'

This wasn't the time to ask him if there was some way he could raise the finance to out-manoeuvre Neville and his cronies—not while he was obviously so worried about something else.

'You don't need to say a word—your very silence condemns you,' he muttered thickly. 'God, when I think how I let you deceive me. How easily I believed.' He swore suddenly and viciously, flinging his glass into the fireplace where it smashed into a million tiny shards.

'Saul! Please . . . What is it?'

'Saul . . . Please . . .!' he mimicked with savage hurtfulness. 'Please what? Take you to bed? Sell this place at a knock-down price to your precious cousin?'

He saw the shock mirrored in her eyes and laughed bitterly. 'Oh yes, I know all about it, Lucy. I overheard the pair of you talking . . . or plotting, rather. You never for one moment meant a word of what you've said to me, did you? It was all a game, a ploy to keep me off guard? And to think I actually . . .' She watched the muscles in his jaw lock, too shocked to take in what was happening. It was almost as though she was taking part in a play—something so unreal that she herself could hardly believe what was going on.

'I saw the car and heard your voices. I was just about to come in when I heard Neville asking you for your help. You didn't even hesitate did you, Lucy?'

His voice rippled with contempt and she shivered beneath the lash of it.

'Saul, you don't understand. I had to pretend to go along with Neville to discover what he was doing. How can you believe I would actually help him to injure you? Is that why you're so angry?' Because of what you thought you overheard?'

'If it was all for my benefit, why haven't you said anything?' he asked her curtly.

Exasperation and pain twisted inside her. 'Because I thought you already had enough on your mind ... because I was worried that you might have had bad news from home and I didn't want to add to it. I was going to tell you, Saul, you must believe that.' For the first time she allowed panic to invade her voice. 'I was going to ask you if it might be possible for you to raise enough interest and funds among your father's business acquaintances to develop the house along the lines Neville was planning yourself. Saul, please, you must believe me.'

He looked at her bleakly and then demanded, 'Why?'

'Because I love you.'

It took all her courage to say it, but she sensed that her words had got through to him. He watched for several minutes, studying her as though weighing up one set of facts against another. She could understand him feeling angry and betrayed if he had only caught the tail part of her conversation with Neville—as he must have done; and what had happened in the past must have only reinforced that feeling of betrayal, but surely he must realise how she felt about him. It hurt her that he should so easily believe her capable of deceit and she was forced to recognise how little they really knew of one another as people.

'Tell me exactly what Neville said,' he demanded at last.

Slowly, almost hesitantly at first, her voice still betraying the shock his accusation had given her, she did so, conscious that all the time he was watching her, almost broodingly. Thinking what?

She longed to cry out to him to believe her but pride prevented her. Something extremely precious and fragile had been shattered by his harsh words and she wasn't sure if it could ever be replaced, and then suddenly his expression changed, his voice faintly husky as he muttered,

'Lucy, for God's sake, don't look at me like that. I apologise for what I said to you. Please try to understand; seeing the two of you together, listening to him talking to you, took me back twelve years. I was jealous,' he told her simply, the words half muffled as his lips moved against her hair. 'So jealous that I didn't stop to think beyond what I'd heard. So jealous, in fact, that I drove away again and took solace in the village pub—at least until I saw Neville's car drive past the window.

'Say you forgive me?' He was kissing her now, fever-hungry kisses that burned into her face and throat.

Reluctantly she pushed him away.

'I came here to have dinner,' she reminded him.

'I don't want dinner—I just want you.'

The controlled man of the previous evening was gone, she realised as she looked into his eyes, spears of mingled fear and joy shafting through her body as she realised what he meant.

'I want you Lucy,' he reinforced, murmuring the words against her mouth. 'Now.'

Caution warred with desire. She remembered the glass of whisky he had hurled against the fireplace. How many had there been before that? Was his desire fuelled by love or something darker? And most important of all, did he really believe what she had told him? He had accepted her explanation readily enough—too readily perhaps in view of his earlier almost frenzied rage.

'Don't you want me?'

His voice whispered tormentingly against her ear, making her shiver with delight. Of course she wanted him. His hand cupped her face, lifting it so that he could look into her eyes.

'You know I do.' Her voice shook slightly.

'Then come with me now.'

Taking her hand he led her slowly out of the room and towards the stairs. They climbed them side by side in silence, all the time her heart thudding heavily against her breastbone. Last night she had tormented her fevered brain with the erotic imaginings of this moment, never dreaming that when it came she would feel more frightened than aroused.

At the top of the stairs Saul stopped to look at her, his eyes dark and shuttered. What did he see when he looked at her? What was he really thinking behind that shuttered exterior? She reached out towards him, suddenly nervous and uncertain, her fingers brushing his arm. The sombreness in his eyes shattered, melting in the heat that sprang to life within them, his arms came round her, lifting her, his mouth hot as it touched her throat.

'Forget about this afternoon,' he muttered thickly against her skin as he carried her into his bedroom. 'Forget everything but how you feel about me and how I feel about you.'

He lowered her on to the bed, the mattress depressing slightly beneath her weight. He was using the room which had belonged to her parents, but no ghosts intruded on them as Saul slowly removed her clothes and then, without taking his eyes from her, his own.

The movement of his hands against her skin was music translated into feelings. Her mouth parted eagerly to the gently insistent pressure of his, her arms locking round him as gentleness gave way to passion.

His hand cupped her breast, his lips trailing most, tender kisses down towards it, delicately caressing the deeply pink tip until he felt her tense beneath him as she fought to subdue the fierce clamour of need within her that demanded more, much more from him than mere tenderness.

As though he knew how his delicacy was tormenting her his mouth opened over the hardened centre of her breast, his tongue arousingly abrasive as it stroked her sensitive skin. The tiny cries of pleasure she could no longer hold inside her chest seemed to fuel his passion as his mouth moved with fierce need from one aroused nipple to the other and then to the moist valley in between, trailing a line of hungry kisses from her breastbone down to where the delicate swell of her womanhood was covered in fine, silky hairs.

There he stopped, registering the shudder rippling through her, the thumb of the hand he had curled possessively round her thigh softly stroking against her skin as he raised his head to look into her eyes.

She wanted to tell him that he was rushing into intimacy too fast but the soft movement of his thumb against her flesh was sending conflicting signals to her brain, overwhelming shyness and shock, making her breathe with odd, jerky little movements that mirrored the hurriedly uneven rise and fall of his chest.

He moved, releasing her abruptly, only to pull her down into his arms, his mouth moving urgently against hers, as he muttered thickly, 'Make love to me, Lucy. Show me that you want me as much as I want you.'

In his thick, almost incoherent plea she recognised the insecure boy he had been that summer twelve years ago, fearing rejection and mockery, and her arms tightened convulsively around him, all her love for him welling up inside her as she touched her lips adoringly to the side of his throat and then more wantonly as she felt his uncontrolled response.

He possessed a sensuality she had never dreamed existed, never even known before, teaching her the pleasure that came from the movement of his tongue against her skin, and the pleasure she herself could take from caressing his

in the same way, feeling the hard muscles
contract beneath his flesh as she touched the
warm skin of his chest.

'Torment me, would you?'

His voice was thick with pleasure as he growled
the words mock-threateningly, his hands sliding
possessively over her back until they cupped the
rounded fullness of her bottom, pulling her
against and into the hardness of his thighs.

The sensation of his aroused body moving
seductively against her skin while she herself was
not allowed to move was tormentingly erotic, and
although Saul pretended that the frantic wriggling
of her upper half as she fought to break free was
angering him, it wasn't anger that gleamed out of
his eyes as his head bent and his mouth captured
the peak of one soft breast.

Feeling the drag of his teeth against her super-
sensitive skin, Lucy moaned, throwing her head
back and arching her spine so that her body
moved eagerly against his, her head thrashing
wildly from side to side as she fought to subdue
the aching need burning through her.

She felt Saul's hand against her thigh and
then shuddered convulsively as he stroked her
moist, eager flesh with tenderness and skill. A
fierce spasm of pleasure gripped her, and she
cried out despairingly to Saul, gripping his
shoulders in her frantic need to feel him deep
inside her.

Her eyes tightly closed, her body rigid with the
aching need she was fighting to control, Lucy felt
him move, cool air shafting momentarily against
her skin and she shuddered with relief, antici-

pating the heated weight of him between her thighs, his body joining hers, filling it.

Only it wasn't the male weight of Saul's body she felt moving against her, but the skilled and delicate stroke of his tongue as it adored her body in that most intimate of all lovers' embraces.

She cried out against this intimacy—her mind shocked by it even while her body voluptuously enjoyed it. Her hands reached down to push him away, and then curled protestingly into the dark thickness of his hair. But it was too late to push him away, too late to do anything other than give in to her body's shameless response to the pleasure he was giving her.

She was still trembling when he took her back in his arms, tucking her head beneath his chin and rocking her gently as he soothed her shaky limbs.

'I wanted to feel you inside me,' she protested tearfully, her voice thick with remembered delight.

She heard him laugh deep in his throat, his breath tickling her ear as he whispered,

'And you most certainly will. That, my darling cousin, was merely our prelude!' She felt him frown against her skin as he added softly, 'For a woman of twenty-five you're deliciously in-experienced.'

She tensed in his arms, and as though he knew what she was thinking he added, 'I'm not fishing, Lucy. Whatever happened in the past is past, but it's a tremendous boost to a man's ego when he knows he's given a woman a pleasure she's never known before.'

She didn't ask him how he had known, but shivered a little, wondering what he would say when he discovered . . . But, no, she wasn't going to think about that now. It wasn't important, hadn't he just told her so?

If she had been inclined to believe that his comment that they would make love had merely been made in jest, she soon realised that she was wrong.

The exhaustion which had gripped her in the aftermath of pleasure turned to languor beneath his slowly seductive kisses, and languor to a fine-tuned desire that increased in urgency as his hands caressed her skin—surely now more sensitive even than before to the slow drift of his fingers.

She in turn caressed him, thrilled and almost a little frightened by the maleness of him and the desire she could feel pounding through his body.

This time she had no need to cry out how much she needed him. He seemed to sense exactly the right moment, moving tantalisingly over, then within her, almost teasingly at first, until he felt the fine tension gripping her body. Then he moved differently, making her gasp in surprised shock. The same shock was registered in his eyes as well she saw, as her own opened wide, but already that sharp, unexpected pain had faded, giving way to urgency and the clamour of her senses. Instinctively she kept him within her, wrapping herself round his body, feeling the faint shudder of desire that seized his muscles, and his shock, like hers, gave way to need, desire escalating between them until it reached an unbearable pinnacle to shatter like fragile glass against the pressure of an almost unreachable high note.

This time he didn't wrap her in his arms. Instead, leaning up on one elbow to study her face, frowning slightly, his voice terse, he asked, 'Why didn't you tell me?'

After his earlier words this was not the reaction she had expected. Avoiding his eyes she shrugged and said quietly, 'It didn't seem important.'

'Important enough,' he responded drily. 'There can't be many twenty-five-year-old virgins around.'

His words hurt and to cover her hurt she said flippantly, 'And now there's one less.'

'Why did you let me make love to you, Lucy?' he asked coldly, without responding. 'Did you think it would convince me that you weren't lying about Neville? Will you tell him about this?' he added before she could speak.

Her body went cold, chilled both by what he was saying and the distant, unemotional tone of his voice. It seemed impossible that they were having this conversation. Less than three hours ago he had been telling her he loved her and now he was acting almost as though he hated her. It was because of her virginity, she thought bitterly . . . Because he didn't love her at all but had simply wanted her, and had been shocked to discover that he was her first lover. No doubt he was scared that she would expect some form of commitment from him, so he was trying to freeze her off in this despicable way.

'Why should I want to discuss what happened

between us with Neville?' she asked him coldly.
'He's my business partner—nothing more.'

The moment she voiced the lie she wanted to
retract it, but Saul was looking down at her with
burning, bitter eyes, his mouth curling into
biting contempt as he said thickly,

'So you *were* lying. You *were* in league with
him all the time. And this was just a way of
softening me up wasn't it, Lucy? Wasn't it?'

He was shaking her now, his fingers biting
painfully into her upper arms.

'You always were easily fooled, Saul,' she told·
him icily. 'I had to tell you what Neville had
planned when you said you'd overheard us, but
of course, I'd never any intention of changing
sides. How on earth could *you* raise the money to
fund such a project?'

'And money of course means everything to
you. I should have known that from the start . . .
all that soft soap about regretting what your
father had done. No doubt you were right there
with him, planning every step. Well I've got news
for you, my dear cousin. I could buy and sell this
place a hundred times over.' He saw her
expression and laughed savagely. 'Oh yes, that
shocks you, doesn't it and you don't want to
believe me, but it's true, I assure you. My
stepfather is a multi-millionaire; and what I
didn't tell you before was that, when he and my
mother married, my father agreed that he could
adopt me legally as his son. Now that he's retired
I run his business empire for him, and I'm a·
wealthy man in my own right, from what I've
learned from him, Lucy. So you see, my dear,

you'd have been much better off casting in your lot with me. What a pity you were so impetuous and so greedy.'

'But then you knew that all along, didn't you,' she said wildly. 'Right from the start you . . .'

'I wondered what you'd be like,' he agreed curtly, 'but you're wrong about one thing. I'm obviously a lot more gullible than I knew because for a while there you had me convinced. I came very close to falling in love with you, Lucy. Too bad I had to overhear that conversation today, otherwise you could have had my millions to play with instead of Neville's thousands. Now get out,' he told her brutally, turning his back on her. 'I'm going to go and have a shower—I want to wash the scent and feel of you off my skin before it pollutes me. When I come back I don't want to find you here. Oh, and you can tell your cousin that he's got absolutely no chance of buying this place . . . no chance at all. I wouldn't like to be in your shoes when you do, Lucy. He looks like a man who has a cruel streak to me.'

He got off the bed and walked towards the door, pausing to turn round and demand thickly, 'For God's sake, what is it about him that you can't resist? He doesn't even want you—any fool can see that . . . He hasn't even made love to you . . . But then having done so myself, I can see why. At least cerebrally it was satisfying— knowing that I was cheating you just as much as you were cheating me.'

He was gone; the door had slammed behind him, but instead of getting dressed she was still sitting up in his bed shivering violently, no longer trying to control the wild tide of tears flooding her eyes.

It was shock, she told herself numbly as she sought to dress herself and control her palsied limbs, shock that made her shake like this and believe that it was all a bitter dream. He could not have said those things to her—not Saul. But he had . . . smashing her dreams and her life, and it would do no good to tell him that he was wrong, so wrong about her feelings for Neville because he would never believe her now. And even if he did . . . He had come near to falling in love with her, he had said, but she didn't believe that. He had suspected her right from the start; he had been waiting for her to make a mistake; and he had deliberately allowed her to think . . . to think that he cared about her, while all the time he had been waiting to trap her.

She was dressed. All she had to do was to walk out. It was the longest walk she ever made, and for ever afterwards she never knew how she managed to get back to the Dower House.

Once there she curled up in a chair downstairs, too shocked and distraught to even think of sleep. On her skin the scent of Saul remained elusive and tantalising, but she didn't even have the energy to go upstairs and wash. She would never see him again. She was determined on that. She had too much pride . . . and too much fear, she acknowledged weepily. If she stayed, how could she stop herself from begging him to believe the truth? She loved him, but he had never loved her, she reminded herself. He had pretended to, yes, but that was all it had been: a pretence. Perhaps he had even come over here with the deliberate intention of hurting her, of getting back at her for his own pain all those years ago.

At last, exhausted and muddled by increasingly miserable thoughts, she fell asleep.

CHAPTER SEVEN

'BUT Lucy, what do you mean, you're going away?'

She and Fanny faced one another across the drawing-room carpet. Fanny had returned from her holiday that morning, looking glowingly tanned and relaxed. In contrast she looked pale, and almost ill, Lucy recognised, but that scarcely mattered. What did was that she had to get away ... from this house ... from its too-close proximity to Saul, who fortunately she hadn't seen since that disastrous evening ten days ago.

'I mean I've decided I want to have a chance to write,' Lucy told her. 'I need peace and quiet to work, Fanny, and that's impossible living here with you and the children.'

As she had anticipated Fanny looked both affronted and hurt, but she wasn't going to allow herself to be dissuaded; she knew exactly what she was going to do.

She hadn't wasted the days before Fanny's return. A phone call to Beverley explaining that she wanted to be in London the better to do some research on her second novel—some of which was to be set in the city—had elicited the information that Beverley knew of a senior editor with another firm who had been seconded to New York for twelve months and who was desperately looking for the right sort of tenant for her flat—

and one who would be willing to look after her Siamese cat.

A quick dash up to London and lunch with the other woman had convinced them both that they had found exactly what they were looking for. Lucy had enough money of her own to be able to live in the flat, if only frugally, without touching any of her capital—she was a first-rate typist and if need be could always augment her income in that way since she was determined not to touch a penny of Oliver's or Tara's.

She had even been to see Mr Patterson to explain her intentions to him, telling him quite firmly that she could not spend the rest of her life looking after two children who already had a mother.

If it turned out that Saul intended to keep the Manor House, which in view of his revelations about his wealth was entirely possible, then she was going to sell the Dower House, but she was keeping this to herself for the time being.

One telephone call which had given her a good deal of pleasure had been the one she had made to Neville to tell him crisply and concisely exactly why his own plans were doomed to failure. He hadn't been pleased, but his bile had barely touched her. She was beyond feeling almost anything now . . . beyond even the pain of Saul's cruel rejection.

'But Lucy . . . we need you,' Fanny wailed.

'No you don't,' Lucy responded reasonably. 'You could always employ an au pair to keep an eye on the children, Fanny. Oliver starts school in the autumn and Tara's no trouble.'

'But this place is so isolated. I'll be lonely.'

'Then buy something closer to town,' Lucy said reasonably. 'I'm sure if you approached Mr Patterson he'd release enough of Oliver's capital for you to do that.'

'But Lucy, you don't understand. Your father wanted Oliver to stay here ... in what is his rightful home.'

'Then my father should have made proper arrangements for him to do so,' Lucy told her crisply, suddenly tired of the demands that were made on her in the name of duty. Her father had never really loved her, not as he loved Oliver, and why should she sacrifice herself in order to virtually bring up his son? She would go mad if she had to stay here much longer, haunted day and night by the memory of the way Saul had looked at her, tormented by memories of how he had touched her ... seduced her into believing he loved her. She shuddered now, fighting to break free of the powerful mental images.

'It's all decided, Fanny,' she went on firmly. 'I'm leaving at the end of the week.'

As though she realised that she couldn't be swayed Fanny went silent.

She would miss the children, Lucy acknowledged later in the week, surveying the growing pile of boxes stacked on the study floor. But she couldn't stay here. So far she had been lucky—she had seen no sign of Saul. Only she knew how, during those first awful days, she had hoped to hear his car outside, his footsteps across the floor, hope slowly withering and then dying as the hours went by without any indication from him that it had all been some terrible mistake and that he loved her after all.

She could only presume now that he was deliberately keeping out of sight and her pride would not allow her to stay somewhere where she was so obviously unwanted—and so vulnerable.

He had been so willing to believe the worst of her—had wanted to believe it, she was convinced now. Perhaps he had engineered the whole situation simply to get back at her, had deliberately and callously set out to make her fall in love with him, while not caring the least about her at all. And then, when he had discovered he was her first lover, he had been too shocked to conceal his true feelings: his lack of desire to have any sort of permanent relationship with her. She would probably never know the whole truth—nor did she want to, she told herself firmly. It was over—for good.

She had to make several journeys to London with her things, her car being too small to transport them all in one go. If and when she sold the Dower House she would have to find somewhere to store her furniture—or get rid of it. Perhaps her uncle might agree to store some of it for her; he and her aunt had a massive Victorian riverside house with plenty of storage space.

Thinking of her uncle reminded Lucy that it was some time since she had seen him, and also that he had no idea of her new address.

Now that he was semi-retired he worked from home, so on the first day of her new life in London she set out to see him.

As always her aunt and uncle were delighted to see her, her aunt kissing her warmly and chiding her for leaving it so long between visits as she drew her into the house.

Margaret Summers clucked anxiously over Lucy's pale face as she ushered her into the sunny room where her husband worked.

'Look who's here, Leo,' she exclaimed as she opened the door.

'Lucy—my dear.'

Leo Summers hugged his niece warmly, noticing as his wife had done that she looked far too fine-drawn and pale.

He had never truly taken to the man his beloved sister had married and it was his private opinion that as a father he had left much to be desired. Mind you, love and caring did not always produce a happy child, as he knew. Their own son Neville was a bitter disappointment to him; to both of them really, although Margaret always remained tremendously loyal to their only child. Perhaps if they had been able to have more as they had planned... As always when he thought about his son, his eyes clouded a little.

'Come and tell us what you're doing with yourself,' Margaret insisted, correctly reading the look in her husband's eyes.

'Well I've left the Dower House and I'm working in London.' As Lucy had anticipated this bombshell provoked an avalanche of questions.

'I never agreed with the way your father expected you to take on the responsibility of Fanny and the children,' Leo said when she had finished. 'But Lucy, you've always loved the country so much. Why didn't you come to us instead of finding a flat? You know we'd have loved to have you.'

'I'm twenty-five years old,' she reminded him wryly, 'and it's time I stood on my own two feet.'

'Umm . . . Well at least I hope we'll see a little more of you now. How about the book; how is it going?'

They talked about her work for half an hour while Margaret went to make some coffee. When she came back there were four cups on the tray instead of three and she looked slightly apprehensive.

'It must be our day for visitors,' she told her husband. 'Neville has just arrived.'

Lucy didn't miss the way her uncle's face tightened at the mention of his son's name, but before he could say anything Neville himself came sauntering into the room.

'Well well, cousin Lucy,' he drawled, eyeing her mockingly. 'What brings you here?'

'Your parents,' she told him evenly, refusing to let him bait her. She knew quite well that he would still be angry with her over the sale of the Manor.

'Lucy's decided to move to London,' his father told him.

'Really?' There was a distinct look of curiosity in his eyes as he studied her. 'A sudden decision I take it?'

'Not really. It's something I've been thinking of for a while.'

'And what will you do with the Dower House, when Saul sells?' he asked her.

'It isn't decided yet that he will.'

'No? It seems pretty conclusive to me. He's gone back to America and according to that cleaning woman he employs he's made no plans to come back. Fanny hasn't seen or heard from him. He's gone for good by the looks of it.'

Gone . . . Saul was gone.

The coffee cup she had just picked up seemed like a dead weight in her hands. She couldn't believe what she was hearing. She wanted to cry out in protest that Saul wouldn't leave without telling her, but everything seemed to be shifting out of focus around her; she tried to cry out and found that her vocal chords seemed to be paralysed. A strange roaring sound engulfed her, the blackness into which she was falling punctuated by her aunt's sharp cry, and then nothing . . .

She came round to find she was lying on the *chaise longue* in her uncle's study. There was no sign of Neville but her aunt and uncle were both hovering anxiously beside her.

'Lucy, my dear, thank goodness. We were just about to send for the doctor. How are you feeling?'

'Fine . . . I'm fine. There's no need to send for anyone,' Lucy protested, trying to sit up and finding weakly that she could not. 'It was just a faint.'

'Maybe . . . It is a warm day, and of course you must have been shocked to learn that Saul intends to sell the house without so much as discussing it with you, but my dear, you look so thin and fine-drawn . . . I really . . .'

Firmly Lucy brushed aside her aunt's concern, assuring her that she was perfectly all right, and at last, although unwillingly, that lady gave in.

'Very well, but I absolutely insist that you spend the night here at the very least.'

Lucy shook her head. 'I'm afraid I can't.' Quickly she explained about Pasha, her feline charge.

'A Siamese! I've always loved them,' her aunt exclaimed. 'Well that's no problem. He can stay as well.'

She wanted to protest, to insist that she was perfectly all right, but all at once it required too much effort. It would be lovely to stay here and be pampered by her aunt. Knowing she was being weak, but totally unable to stop herself, Lucy gave her uncle instructions as to how to find her flat, handing him the key while her aunt gave him instructions as to what Lucy and Pasha would need.

To tell the truth she hadn't been feeling well for the past few days. Initially she had put her inertia and lack of desire to eat down to the fact that she was too wrought up over her quarrel with Saul, but as the days had gone by and her appetite had continued to desert her a heavy listlessness had seemed to envelop her.

It was delicious to simply lie back and be saved the necessity of making any decision, of doing anything other than be pampered. That alone told Lucy how seriously depleted her physical and emotional resources must be. Normally she was so independent and self-reliant. For some reason she felt acutely weepy, gladly accepting

Margaret's suggestion that she simply lie quietly in the cool of the study until her uncle got back.

In the event, what was to have been merely an overnight stay stretched into nearly a week, with Margaret resolutely stating that she was far from well enough to be living alone and Lucy weakly giving in and enjoying her aunt's cosseting.

It was a long time since she had been so thoroughly spoiled, the calm atmosphere of the riverside house and the placidness of its two semi-elderly inhabitants having a beneficial effect on her over-stretched nerves.

If it wasn't for the lassitude that continued to envelop her Lucy thought she might have felt more inclined to make a move back to her flat, but every time she said as much she found herself thoroughly overruled.

When she remarked to her uncle one morning that she felt very guilty for causing her aunt so much work, he replied with a twinkle in his eyes that Margaret was enjoying keeping busy.

'She looks on you as the daughter she never had, Lucy,' he told her. 'And as for that cat!'

If Lucy was enjoying the spoiling then so was Pasha. The Siamese had quickly discovered a devoted slave in Margaret, and one moreover who was willing to feed him on such delicacies as fresh salmon instead of the canned food which was his normal fare.

Every day he accompanied Margaret on her tour of her garden, padding delicately over the grass with a proudly disdainful air before returning to join Lucy in the study.

When it had become clear that her stay was

going to be more than an overnight one, her uncle had returned to the flat to collect her papers and notebooks, and most afternoons Lucy made an attempt to get down to work, although an attempt was usually all it was.

This morning she had been ferociously nauseous after breakfast, for the second day running, and she was now lying outside in the garden, shaded by an umbrella, watching her aunt deadhead her roses.

As she eyed her aunt's stooping back Lucy knew there was something that could not be put off any more.

When Margaret straightened and suggested, 'Coffee?' she held out her hand.

'In a minute. There's something I have to tell you first. I think I might be pregnant.'

She said it abruptly, wondering if her aunt would be as shocked as she had been when she first began to suspect the reason for her continued lassitude and sickness. She hated having to hurt her aunt with such an announcement but her own honesty forced her to admit it. She could not continue to remain under her uncle's roof being pampered and indulged like a Victorian invalid when she was really nothing of the sort.

'Yes, I suspected as much.'

The calm acceptance in her aunt's voice made her lift startled brown eyes to Margaret's placid blue ones.

'You knew?'

'I recognised the signs,' Margaret told her wryly. 'I suffered a very similar tiredness with Neville, and then again later with the one I lost.'

'You must have wondered why I didn't say anything, but until the other day it never occurred to me . . . That is . . .'

Her aunt sat down at her side, taking hold of her hand.

'Lucy, you're an adult woman, and the world has changed a good deal since I was a girl. Even so, I don't see you as someone who would want to bring a child into the world outside marriage and with no father to help care for it.'

'I'm not,' Lucy agreed. 'Much as I hate to admit it, I've behaved as irresponsibly as a teenager, never even giving a thought to the consequences. Worse than a teenager,' she added wryly. 'Nowadays I think they're far more sensible than I've been.'

'I take it that there's no chance of you and the father . . .' Margaret probed delicately, stopping when she saw the bright flash of tears in her niece's eyes as she shook her head.

'He knows nothing about this, Margaret, nor would he want to know. I thought he loved me, but I know now that he doesn't; I'm on my own in this.'

'No you're not,' Margaret told her gently, 'you have your uncle and myself.'

Lucy gave her a watery smile.

'That's sweet of you, but I must leave now, Margaret, I can't embarrass you and Uncle Leo by staying. There's bound to be gossip.'

'So what?' The grey eyebrows arched faintly. 'We might be getting on in years, Lucy, but we aren't completely behind the times. An illegitimate baby these days is nothing and what gossip there is will quickly die down. You don't think your uncle and I would let you live alone now, do you? No . . . you're staying here.'

It was so unusual to hear her gentle aunt speaking so firmly that Lucy was silenced.

'I take it that you intend to continue with the pregnancy?'

'As opposed to an abortion? Yes.' Right from the moment two days ago when she had realised she must be pregnant Lucy had known she would keep the child—Saul's child. Already, despite her shock, the thought of the baby soothed the ache in her heart. Becoming pregnant was not something she would have chosen to do, but now that she was she discovered she was not as unhappy at the thought as she might have been.

'You must see Dr Carter now,' Margaret informed her. 'I'll give him a ring tomorrow and get him to come round.'

'Margaret, before you make any plans I must tell Uncle Leo. He might not feel the same way as you do.'

'He does,' Margaret further stunned her by saying. 'We've already discussed it, Lucy,' she told her niece. 'You see, almost from the start I suspected what might be wrong. Leo wants you and your baby here just as much as I do.'

She saw the glitter of tears darkening Lucy's eyes and with a small murmur went to her and put her arms round her, wisely knowing that it was best to let her cry.

'I promise you we won't ask any questions,' she said later when they were drinking their coffee, but Lucy shook her head firmly.

'No . . . If I'm going to stay here with you, you should know the truth.'

It was at the back of her mind that since her pregnancy could not be kept a total secret it was inevitable that if her aunt and uncle did not know who the father was, they could quite innocently mention it to Fanny, from whom it might get back to Saul—always supposing he returned from the States—and that was the last thing she wanted to happen. If he learned about the child, Saul might feel he was under some sort of obligation towards it—and possibly to her—and she didn't want that. If she couldn't have his love, then she didn't want anything from him.

Margaret listened silently as Lucy went briefly through what had happened, carefully editing Neville's role in the affair.

'He was so shocked to discover that he was my first lover that I knew then that he didn't love me.'

'Lucy, are you sure? You could be wrong. It seems to me that you almost deliberately encouraged him to believe the worst of you.'

'But if he had loved me he wouldn't have believed it, would he?' she protested.

Margaret sighed. 'Perhaps not, but human emotions are tricky things, my dear, and from what you've said to me it seems as though he would be bitterly resentful of any part Neville played in your life. People in love are notorious for not behaving in a logical fashion. Given the past, perhaps he was just testing you . . . hoping you would deny his accusations.'

Could her aunt be right? Lucy stamped firmly

on the frail seed of hope burgeoning inside her. Saul had made no attempt to get in touch with her or show any interest in her at all since that fateful night. No, her aunt was wrong. He cared nothing about her at all.

That evening over dinner her uncle suggested that for the time being they keep the news of Lucy's pregnancy to themselves.

'Not because we're ashamed or embarrassed, Lucy, but simply so that you're not subject to unwanted questions. I suggest that, when the time comes, we'll invent some fictitious father for the child, but we'll think about that later.'

Later when Lucy was in bed and he and his wife were alone in the privacy of their own bedroom Margaret asked her husband anxiously, 'Leo, what are we going to do? Lucy, poor child, looks worn to a thread. She loves him desperately, you know, and she's far too proud to do anything about it.'

'Yes I know, and she won't thank us for any interference. I suppose old Patterson the solicitor would be the person most likely to have his American address? I'll give him a ring in the morning.'

'And if Lucy's right and Saul doesn't want her or the baby?'

'Then his loss is our gain, isn't it?'

'Fanny's on the phone for you,' Margaret announced to Lucy a couple of days later. 'She sounds very excited.'

Dr Carter had confirmed that Lucy was indeed

pregnant, and although the nausea continued her exhaustion seemed to be lifting. She went into the study to pick up the receiver.

'Lucy, you'll never guess ... I'm getting married again!' The excitement faded from the bubbly light voice as Fanny quite obviously remembered that her deceased husband had been Lucy's father, but Lucy wasn't at all upset by her news, especially when she learned that Fanny was to marry their neighbour and friend, the colonel.

'He proposed to me at the weekend—we won't have a long engagement, only a couple of months. Oliver and Tara are both delighted, and I must confess that it will be a relief to share the responsibility for them with someone else again.

'We're having a small engagement party this weekend at his house and, of course, we both want you to be there. The children miss you.'

Of course she couldn't refuse to go, and besides what was there to stop her from attending? After all, Saul wasn't going to be there.

CHAPTER EIGHT

'WELL that went off very well didn't it?'

Lucy, her aunt and her uncle were in the drawing-room of the Dower House, drinking the chocolate her aunt had insisted on making on their return from the engagement party.

Fanny and the two children were spending the weekend at Tom's house, and Lucy had been pleased to see how well both children, but especially Oliver, got on with him.

Before she left Tom had taken her on one side to tell her that he knew all about Oliver's true parentage.

'To be honest, I had wondered. He has a look of your father. I think Fanny should tell him the truth and as soon as possible, but she doesn't agree with me—at least not yet.'

Lucy did though and she had told him so. The sooner Oliver knew the truth the less traumatic it would be for him, and she had every faith in Tom's ability to make Fanny see the wisdom of telling him.

Conventional to the last, Fanny was insisting on waiting until she had been a widow for a full year before she and Tom married, which meant that Lucy would have to shelve her plans for putting the Dower House on the market, she decided as she prepared for bed. Her aunt and uncle had assured her that she would always have a home with them, but she felt that she could not stay cocooned in their protective love for ever. Before the baby was born she would have to come to some decision about their future. If she sold the Dower House, she could buy something smaller and invest the remainder of the money to bring in a small income—but would that be enough for them to live on? Her book would, hopefully, bring her in some additional income. She wanted to be independent, she realised, as she lay sleepless in her bed. She wanted to prove that she was capable of supporting herself and her child. But to whom? Saul?

Even thinking his name was like a sword in her flesh, the pain almost unendurable.

She was awake early—too alert to go back to sleep, but reluctant to disturb her aunt and uncle whom she knew enjoyed a well deserved lie-in on Sunday mornings.

Outside, the sun shone, dispersing the faint mist hanging over the distant hollows in the landscape; an early warning that summer was waning and autumn was on the way.

Autumn was normally one of her favourite seasons, but now she contemplated its faintly melancholy nostalgia that mourned the loss of summer with more acute sensitivity. Shivering a little she got up and dressed, hurrying downstairs to the kitchen to make herself a cup of coffee.

When she had drunk it, an impulse she knew she ought to master but could not urged her outside, her feet automatically taking her along the familiar path to the Manor.

She had walked this drive more times than she

cared to remember, but this morning the only journeys she remembered making along it were those which had taken her to Saul.

The house stood, as it had always stood, solid and impervious, but for once she looked at it without seeing all the countless generations of people who had lived within its walls and instead saw only herself and Saul. Like someone unable to resist the lure of something known to be dangerous, she walked towards the house. The front door was open and yielded easily to her touch, but there was nothing odd in that—it was rarely locked.

Inside, the hall had that cold desolateness of houses without inhabitants. The bowl for flowers which had always graced the hall table was gone, a faint film of dust coating the mahogany surface.

Slowly Lucy walked into the drawing-room, mentally reliving the moment when she had found Saul here and he had accused her of plotting against him with Neville. There had been a time immediately after their quarrel when she had hoped that his cruel words to her had been the result of anger and jealousy caused by this belief, but she knew that if that had been the case he would have come looking for her once his anger had cooled.

The very fact that he had not proved beyond any doubt that he had never really loved her. She could have forgiven those cruel, hurtful words of his if she thought they had been flung at her in the heat of the moment and then regretted— loving him as she did she could well imagine herself reacting in a very similar way had their positions been reversed—but Saul hadn't reacted in anger and primitive jealousy. He had acted callously and cold-bloodedly, wanting to hurt and destroy her.

She shivered, placing a protective hand against her stomach. Whatever else happened, she was not going to allow her child to suffer for its father's omissions. Her child. Saul's child ... A child who would never know its father.

'Lucy.'

For a moment she was sure she must be hallucinating, imagining that the voice she heard was Saul's, and then she turned round and saw that she was not.

He was standing less than ten feet away from her, just inside the door, his arms hanging loosely at his sides, his face oddly sharp-boned.

She swallowed, fighting down an insane urge to rush into his arms, and then as he took a step towards her, her composure shattered completely and she stepped back, her whole world exploding in shock and pain as she realised that he was real, that he was actually here, speaking to her as unemotionally as though they were nothing more than distant cousins.

The now familiar wall of blackness roared up around her, her last thought as faintness rushed sickeningly over her that she must somehow contrive to stop behaving like the heroine of a Victorian novelette. Fainting was the coward's way out, and ridiculously over-dramatic ... but very, very effective, she thought tiredly as the darkness overwhelmed her completely; very, very effective.

*   *   *

When she came round she was lying on a sofa, her legs raised slightly by the cushions.

As she struggled to remember what had happened, Saul's voice from somewhere behind her right ear announced curtly,

'I've sent for the doctor; he should be here soon.'

She panicked then, trying to sit up and assure him that she was perfectly all right, both at the same time. The resulting wave of sickness that engulfed her warned her of the folly of trying to do anything too abruptly. She felt extraordinarily weak and shaky, so much so that she said nothing as Saul sprang forward and eased her gently back on to the settee.

'What . . . what are you doing here? I thought you were in America.'

'I was,' he agreed tersely.

'Fanny's going to marry Tom Bishop.'

What a ridiculous thing to be telling him when there was so much between them, Lucy thought wanly, closing her eyes against the mockery she was sure she would see in his. She wanted to get up and run away from him as fast as she could, but she simply did not have the strength.

'You shouldn't have called the doctor,' she told him, 'I'll be all right in a moment. It was just the shock . . .'

'Of seeing me?'

She could hear the derision in his voice and it hurt. She could feel the tears burning behind her eyes.

'Lucy, I . . .'

The rough urgency in his voice made her open

her eyes, but even as she did so they both heard the car outside, and he swore abruptly, striding towards the door.

'This will be the doctor,' he told her from the doorway. 'Don't try to move.'

He was back within seconds, the doctor behind him, but it was not plump, old-fashioned Dr Hartley, who she remembered from her childhood; it was a much younger man, who she realised must be his new partner.

'Well, young lady. What have you been doing to yourself?'

'She fainted,' Saul told him quickly before Lucy could speak. She saw the doctor frown.

'What happened? Did you have a fall? Bump into something?'

Saul was looking at her, and she licked her lips nervously, icy cold fingers of dread stroking chillingly up her spine. The darkness welled sickeningly around her again, and as she succumbed to it, grateful this time for its blanketing protection, she thought she heard Saul swear, his voice sharp with an anxiety she knew very well could not be for her.

This time when she came round she was in bed in her old bedroom at the Manor. The doctor was sitting in the window staring out of it, but as though some sixth sense alerted him to her recovery he turned and smiled reassuringly at her.

'Don't panic. There's nothing really wrong with you . . . just a small vitamin imbalance, I suspect. Something that's relatively common in pregnant women, although in your case . . .' He frowned, and dread turned her heart over inside her.

'You're going to have to take things easy—especially in the last weeks of your pregnancy—no physical or mental exertion of any kind. You're not married I take it?' he asked bluntly.

Lucy shook her head.

'Mmm . . . Anyone who can look after you?'

'My aunt and uncle . . .' Panic overwhelmed her as she demanded huskily, 'My baby . . .'

His expression softened slightly. 'You and your baby will both be fine, just so long as you're sensible,' he assured her. 'But being sensible means not worrying—not rushing about exhausting yourself—especially in the last few weeks of your pregnancy. This particular deficiency can result in a premature birth—something we doctors like to avoid.'

He saw that she was looking thoroughly alarmed and added soothingly, 'However, I'm sure you're going to behave sensibly and there won't be any problems. We'll need to get you into hospital for a couple of days to check just how bad the deficiency is, so that we can decide how we're going to tackle it—in mild cases, oral vitamin supplements are enough; in more serious ones we prefer to give intravenous shots.

'My baby . . .' she asked anxiously.

'Will be fine,' he repeated. 'Just as long as you behave sensibly. Now, are you actually staying here, or . . .'

'At the Dower House,' Lucy told him tiredly. Her fainting attacks and constant tiredness were now taking on a more sinister meaning and she shivered a little despite the warmth of the quilt covering her.

'Mmm. Well I'd prefer not to move you from here for today. I'll come back and see you this afternoon—let you know what arrangements I've made with the hospital. Is there anyone at the Dower House who . . .'

'My aunt,' Lucy told him, thinking how worried her aunt and uncle would be when they woke up and found her missing. What would have happened to her if Saul hadn't appeared? If she had fainted when she was alone . . . But if Saul hadn't turned up she probably would not have fainted in the first place, she told herself staunchly. It was the shock of seeing him that had brought on her paralysing weakness.

Saul! Where was he now? *He* must not find out she was pregnant.

'I'll leave you now,' the doctor told her briskly. 'I advise you to try and get some sleep if you can. I'll pop in and tell your aunt what's happening on my way past. Now remember . . . no worrying.'

She heard the doctor's footsteps dying away, and then the slam of his car door and the rev of an engine as he drove away.

All around her she could hear the familiar creaks and groans of the house, so familiar that she was only half aware of them. Where was Saul? What on earth would he say when he learned she had to stay here . . . at least until this afternoon? She should have told the doctor it wasn't possible, but she had been so concerned about the safety of her baby.

The door opened and Saul walked in carrying a

cup of tea. 'Ellis said you could have this,' he told her abruptly, placing it down within reach of her hand, but then instead of leaving he walked over to the window, staring out of it for several seconds, with his back to her, before swinging round to face her. His forehead was creased in a frown, his eyes sombre and dark grey.

'Lucy, we have to talk,' he announced curtly.

Panic and fear curled protestingly through her stomach. She didn't want to talk; she wanted to run away ... To ... But no, she had to face up to him.

'What about?' she asked coolly, turning her head slightly away from him as she added half under her breath, 'I thought you'd already said it all.'

'Lucy, you know I ... What's past is past,' he told her in a different, colder tone. 'And you know damned well what we have to talk about, so stop playing games, and instead start thinking about the future of our child.'

The harshness in his voice grazed her over-sensitive nerves. She wanted to deny his words, to tell him that the baby was hers, and hers alone, but she was too shocked by what he had said. How had he discovered?

'Don't bother denying it,' he continued. 'When Ellis said you were pregnant, I knew immediately the baby must be mine.'

'Must it?'

His eyes grim, he said cruelly, 'Unless by some miracle you've persuaded Neville to take you to bed, then yes, it must.'

His voice warned her that he wasn't going to

believe any lie she might try to spin him about
Neville being the father of her child. Her head
lifted proudly as she met his glance head on.

'Very well then, Saul,' she agreed tightly. 'The
baby *is* yours—inasmuch as you've fathered it—
but you needn't worry that I shall be making any
claims on you, either now or in the future.'

'You won't have to,' he told her tightly. 'I'll be
right there alongside my son or daughter
watching him or her growing up. You've two
courses Lucy; either you agree to marry me, or I
take you through every court in the land to prove
that I can give our child a far better life than you
could ever manage.'

The shock of it brought her close to fainting
again, but somehow she held on to full
consciousness, her voice so frail she could barely
hear it herself as she demanded huskily,

'But Saul, *why*? There's no reason for you to
make yourself responsible for . . . for what
happened. And if you're so desperate to have
children you . . .'

'Lucy, we've got to try and talk sensibly about
this. Ellis has told me about your vitamin
deficiency.' He saw her expression and said
harshly, 'For God's sake, do you want to lose the
baby?'

Her face gave her away, and she turned her
head so that he wouldn't see the weak tears
flooding her eyes.

She had not wanted Saul to know she had
conceived his child, but she had never, ever
dreamed he would react like this, or that he
would propose marriage. Pain tightened round

her body, encircling her with tormenting fingers. Less than a month ago she would have been overjoyed to receive his proposal, but now . . . He didn't want her, he just wanted . . . What? His child?

'You need proper care and looking after. Living alone . . .'

'I won't be living alone.' She saw the colour drain out of his face, a murderous expression darkening his eyes.

'If you think I'm going to let Summers raise my child . . .'

'This has nothing to do with Neville. I'm talking about his parents, my aunt and uncle. They've offered me a home.'

'But I'm not just offering you a home, Lucy. Think about it. Do you really feel you have the right to reject me on behalf of our child? Children need two parents—I think we both know that. How will our son or daughter feel knowing that . . .'

He broke off as they both heard the front doorbell.

'That will probably be my aunt and uncle, Saul,' she told him tiredly. 'Dr Ellis said he would call at the Dower House.' Her mouth tightened as she added, 'It seems unfair that fate should have brought you back here just at this particular moment. I had no intention of telling you about the baby. Why did you come back anyway? Fanny seemed to think you weren't going to.'

There was a strange expression in his eyes for a moment.

'Did you think I'd gone for ever as well, Lucy?' he asked her, his voice oddly husky.

She turned her head away, unable to bear looking at him any longer. If she did, she was bound to betray her pain, to cry out to him that, despite everything that had happened, she had somehow clung to the hope that he had genuinely cared about her, and that, once his anger had cooled, he would regret their quarrel as much as she had herself.

'I didn't really give it much thought,' she said coolly, punishing herself with her denial of her love.

'No, I suppose you were too busy telling Summers why his little plan wasn't going to come off,' he said harshly. 'By the way,' he added as he walked over to the door, 'I've decided to keep this place after all—my mother says she'd like to come back and see it. She did grow up here when all's said and done, and now that I'm to be a father—who knows, maybe my son or daughter might inherit your father's obsession with the place. Think about it, Lucy,' he said softly from the door. 'Think about all you'll be denying our child, simply for the pleasure of getting at me. Are you really that selfish?'

It was a low blow, and one it took her several seconds to assimilate. Had he really been offering to keep the Manor as a form of bribery, or had she simply allowed her fevered imagination to run away with her?

Marriage to Saul! Once she would have asked nothing more from life, but how could she marry him knowing that he didn't love her; that he was simply marrying her because they had conceived a child?

'You can't want to marry me.'

She said it so quietly, she thought he couldn't have heard, but he must have done, because he turned in the doorway and said softly, 'Can't I? Maybe not. But I promise you I'll do anything, and everything, that's necessary to keep my child away from Summers' influence.'

As he left her his words sank into her mind, leaving her shaken and trembling from head to foot. She was only just beginning to realise how deep the vein of antipathy between the two men ran. As a child she had known it was there, of course, but now as an adult she saw that the schism was much greater than she had perceived. To say they hated one another was perhaps an exaggeration, but it was no exaggeration to say that Neville loathed and detested Saul; and Saul, it seemed, more than returned his feelings—to the extent that he would marry her himself rather than allow his child to be 'contaminated' by any relationship she had with Neville.

Once married to Saul she could see that he would soon put a stop to any relationship between Neville and herself—even a cousinly one. But it was all so futile. She cared nothing for Neville—she didn't even particularly like him. She had told Saul as much.

But she had also told him that she had plotted against him behind his back with Neville, she reminded herself; she had unwittingly fed the resentment Saul felt towards her maternal cousin, not realising how intensely Saul felt about him.

It was perhaps feasible that Saul should think she cared far more for Neville than she actually did, in view of the crush she had had on him when she was twelve.

Her reverie was broken as the door opened to admit her aunt, her plump face creased into worried anxiety.

'Lucy, my dear. How are you feeling? Dr Ellis called at the Dower House and told us . . .'

Saul apparently had opted to stay downstairs.

'He's talking to your uncle,' Margaret told her when Lucy enquired. 'So you're quite safe if you want a private chat.'

As always her aunt's shrewdness caught her off guard. Margaret always looked so naïve that it was a surprise to discover just how on the ball she really was.

'Did Dr Ellis tell you about this vitamin deficiency he thinks I have?'

'He did mention it briefly, yes,' Margaret agreed, frowning again. 'He wants you to go into hospital for some tests, apparently.'

'Yes. He's coming back this afternoon to tell me what arrangements he's made.'

It was plain to Margaret that her niece's mind was on something else, and she looked at her thoughtfully for a second before saying quietly, 'What's really worrying you, Lucy?'

Her aunt's perception brought a vagrant smile to her lips. 'Saul wants us to get married,' she said bluntly. 'He knows about the baby.'

'My dear, you must be so pleased!'

Margaret's reaction was so different from her own that it was several seconds before Lucy could assimilate it. When she had, she smiled a little wryly. Perhaps it was unfair of her after all to expect her aunt to be anything other than a product of her generation and upbringing. To Margaret, the fact that Saul wanted to marry her obviously represented a happy ending to the little saga.

'He doesn't love me, Margaret,' she felt bound to say. 'He simply wants to marry me because . . .' She could hardly tell her aunt of Saul's dislike of Neville, she realised.

'Because he feels it is the right thing to do,' her aunt finished approvingly for her. 'And so it is, Lucy. A child needs two parents,' she reminded her niece, unwittingly echoing Saul's own words. 'I know you must be feeling very muddled and confused, but, my dear, I do urge you to give Saul's proposal proper consideration. Of course your uncle and I would support you in whatever you decide to do, but I really think . . .'

'That I should accept Saul's proposal?'

Suddenly she felt unutterably depressed . . . betrayed almost. She wanted to cry out that she didn't want to marry a man who didn't love her, but somehow she simply did not have the strength, and wouldn't Aunt Margaret perhaps just think her actions selfish? Was she being selfish, in denying her child the opportunity to grow up in the secured, moneyed background Saul could provide for them?

What was the matter with her? she asked herself crossly. How on earth had she become so irresolute and weak? She was behaving more like Fanny than herself; Fanny the clinging vine who was only too happy to entrust her responsibilities to others.

Suddenly she thought of Oliver, growing up under the burden of not knowing the truth about his parentage. Would she honestly want that for her child?

What on earth should she do?

It was a question which worried at her almost constantly over the next two days, wholly taking over that part of her brain which was not occupied with the hospital tests that were being carried out on her.

The private room she had found waiting for her on her arrival at the local hospital had been something of a surprise, and she had queried it, only to discover that she had been given a private room on Saul's instructions.

Already he seemed to be taking over her life, staking a claim in the future of their child.

So far the tests had been very reassuring, and the doctor attending her was convinced that the vitamin deficiency was relatively minor.

'That does not mean of course that it can be ignored,' he told her on the second afternoon of her stay. 'But it does mean that initially we can compensate for it with very small doses of vitamin.

'Mr Bradford informs us that it's more than likely that you and he will be returning to Florida very shortly. That's good. The Americans are very on the ball with their ante-natal care. The sunshine should help as well—it will make you relax a little. You're very tense and on edge. Too much so. It won't do the baby any good, you know.'

'Are you trying to tell me I could have a miscarriage?' Lucy asked frantically, alarmed by the grave expression in his eyes.

'There is always that possibility,' he agreed. 'Not so much due to the vitamin problem as to your own mental state. You need to relax more. You're not sleeping, so the nurses tell me. These first months are often an anxious time, especially with a first baby. Some women can sail through pregnancy, others aren't as lucky. Your health will need to be carefully monitored.'

After he had gone, Lucy lay with her eyes closed, but sleep had never been further away. Did she have the right to risk the life of her baby, simply because she could not endure that thought of Saul marrying her merely out of necessity? Because she wanted love and not duty?

She was told that she could go home the following morning, but that she ought to stay in the area for a few days until all the results of the tests had come through.

In the evening Margaret and Leo both visited her, Leo looking faintly apprehensive and Margaret openly admiring the luxury of her room.

'Goodness, it's more like a luxury hotel bedroom than a hospital,' she commented as she sat down in the chair the nurse provided.

'How are you feeling?' she added, studying Lucy's pale face. 'We saw your doctor on our way in and he says that the vitamin problem isn't too desperate. He is worried about you though, Lucy. He was telling Saul . . .'

'Saul? Saul's here with you?' Instantly she was

thrown into a panic.

'He's with the doctor,' Margaret told her. 'Lucy, have you thought seriously about his offer of marriage?' she asked anxiously. 'Please don't think Leo and I are backtracking on our offer to have you with us, but from what your doctor has been telling us I'm really very concerned about anything happening to you. The house is rather remote, and if Leo and I weren't there and something happened . . . We do go out rather a lot, and we're due to go on holiday with some friends later in the month. I'm not trying to put you off, my dear, but for your sake and the baby's, wouldn't you be better off with Saul? After all, it is his child . . . and you do love him.'

Yes, she did, and that was the problem. If she didn't love him it would be much easier for her to come to a decision, to decide cold-bloodedly and without emotion that Saul owed it to both her and the baby to take care of them; but loving him as she did, it was agonising to contemplate living in some degree of intimacy with him, while knowing that he disliked and despised her, and cared only for their child. Did she have the strength to endure that?

When visiting time came to an end without Saul coming in to see her she was dismayed to discover how disappointed she felt. She told herself it was only because she wanted to discover what he had learned from her doctor, but she knew that wasn't completely true. She wanted to see him, craved the sight of him like a junkie hooked on drugs, even while she knew it destroyed her.

*   *   *

Taking her completely off guard he arrived the next morning, just as she was being discharged. His expression was grim and uncommunicative as he led her to his car.

She had expected her aunt and uncle to come for her, and tiny prickles of apprehension iced up and down her spine as he opened the door for her.

He didn't speak at all as they drove back, only addressing her when, instead of stopping at the Dower House, he swept past it, down the drive towards the Manor.

'Don't worry,' he told her laconically, 'I'm not kidnapping you. I just wanted to have a little talk before I restored you to the bosom of your family.'

Lucy could guess what he wanted to talk about and, drained by the sudden surge of weakness flooding her body, she said tiredly, 'There's no need for us to talk, Saul. You've won. I'll marry you. But please . . . all I want to do right now is lie down . . .'

Her voice wobbled betrayingly, the car screeching to a halt as he almost stood on the brakes halfway down the drive.

At first she thought he was angry with her, and then she realised the tension round his mouth and in his eyes was caused by fear—fear not for her, but for their child, she realised hazily as he leaned towards her, his voice urgent as he called her name, dragging her back from that black place that waited for her.

'Damn, you, Lucy,' he swore thickly, as her faintness receded. 'You take years off my life

every time you do that. Is it any wonder your
aunt and uncle are anxious about you? Have you
thought about what might happen if you blacked
out like that when you were alone?'

Of course she had; almost constantly since
being admitted to hospital; and that was one of
the main reasons she had agreed to marry him. It
was unfair to expect her aunt and uncle to give up
their normal routine simply to be with her
twenty-four hours a day, and that was what the
doctor had warned her was necessary, especially
in these early crucial weeks. But Saul was wealthy
enough to provide round the clock care—
something neither she nor her aunt and uncle
could afford—and, for the sake of her child, she
knew she must accept his proposal.

'Don't nag me, Saul,' she heard herself saying
breathlessly. 'I really can't take it at the moment.
You've got what you wanted; I've agreed to
marry you. Now please take me home.'

Without another word he turned the car round
and drove back to the Dower House.

Of course, he insisted on coming in with her,
and, of course, he had to tell her aunt and uncle
what had happened. Her aunt made no attempt to
hide her delight, although her uncle was more
restrained, more anxiously aware that she looked
both drained and ill.

'You'll stay here until we can be married,' Saul
told Lucy before he left. 'I'll also arrange for a
nurse to stay, to keep an eye on you.' He saw her
expression and added curtly. 'Don't argue with
me, Lucy, it isn't good for you. And if you won't
think of yourself and our child,' his mouth

tightened a little over the words, 'then think of your aunt. It isn't fair to expect her to keep an eye on you twenty-four hours a day, and that's what you need right now.'

She was too exhausted to argue. It was far simpler to give in, to allow her aunt to guide her upstairs and help her into bed. To let sleep claim her and open up an escape route from reality. Saul had taken charge and for once in her life she did not have the strength to object to someone else making her decisions for her.

At the back of her mind lurked the suspicion that this was after all what she wanted. She had wanted to marry Saul all along and, despite discovering that he didn't love her, that desire was still there, and that was partially why she was giving in so easily. Of course she dismissed the thought. The reason she was marrying Saul was because she was being pressured into it, as much by her own fear for the safety of her baby as by her relatives and Saul himself.

CHAPTER NINE

THEY were married very quietly a week later in the small village church. Her aunt and uncle, and Fanny, Tom and the children were their only witnesses.

The only two people who seemed unaware of the undercurrents surrounding the ceremony were Oliver and Tara. The only blot on Tara's blissful delight was the fact that Lucy was not getting married in a traditional white dress and would not therefore require a bridesmaid.

In fact Lucy wore a soft pink silk suit that her aunt bought in London for her; she was too exhausted and emotionally shattered herself to care what she wore.

'At least Neville has had the grace to stay away,' Saul commented curtly as they left the church. 'Or was he motivated more by cowardice than compassion?'

Lucy pressed her lips together, not deigning to answer him. If it pleased him to taunt her about Neville, then let him. It was better by far that he should believe she loved her cousin than that he should guess the truth.

The excuse Saul gave for his parents' non-attendance at the wedding was that his stepfather was still unwell. Lucy hadn't even asked him if his mother knew of their marriage.

In the days leading up to the wedding she had

decided that the only way she could cope with their marriage was for her to distance herself from Saul as much as she could, and that meant not asking him any questions that were in the least personal.

After the ceremony she had to endure the ordeal of the small reception her aunt and uncle had arranged at a local hotel. Her aunt had been shocked by Lucy's suggestion that it was unnecessary, and it was true that although Fanny had glanced rather speculatively at her once or twice, everyone else did seem to be enjoying themselves.

They were due to fly to Florida in the morning. His business responsibilities meant that they would have to live in the States, Saul had told Fanny in response to her surprise.

Lucy shivered faintly, anticipating the loneliness of her new life so far away from everyone she knew. It was true that Saul's mother was her aunt, but that did not alter the fact that they were complete strangers to one another. Would Saul's mother welcome her as a wife for her son? And how would she feel when she discovered that she was carrying Saul's child? Lucy's chin tilted firmly. That was something over which she was determined to allow no deceit. If Saul did not choose to tell his mother that she was pregnant, then she would.

'If those tears are for Summers, you're wasting them.'

The cold incisive voice against her ear made Lucy sit up straighter in her seat, her head

turned defiantly towards the small window of the
jumbo jet.

They had been airborne for about twenty
minutes now, and she felt so battered and
numbed by the speed of recent events that even
now she could barely comprehend that she was
on her way to a new life in a new country.

Fanny, Tom, the two children, and her aunt
and uncle had all come to the airport to see them
off, and strangely she had managed to remain
dry-eyed during that ordeal, pinning a bright
smile to a mouth that seemed permanently
stretched in false gaiety. She had hugged and
kissed Tara, promised Oliver that she would
write to him, suffered Fanny's tearful embrace
with perfect calm and equanimity; but now, when
she was virtually alone with Saul, with no means
of hiding her panic and despair from him, her
self-control had chosen to desert her, causing
tears of shock and misery to slide slowly from her
eyes.

'Here.'

The handkerchief he passed her was soft and
white, his gesture so much at odds with his
harshly derisive tone that she frowned at the
square of white cotton he was handing her for
several seconds before reaching out to take it
from him.

Their fingers touched, the oddest sensation
flowing through her body from that point of
contact. Hot and breathless, she told herself she
was simply suffering the effects of the pressurised
cabin. As she dried her damp face she became
aware that the handkerchief smelled faintly of

Saul's cologne. Her hand started to shake, her breath trapped in her lungs as he suddenly leaned across her.

For a second their eyes met: hers confused and wary, his coolly grey and remote, and then she realised that he was simply releasing her seatbelt for her. For a moment as he leaned towards her she had actually thought . . .

Her cheeks scarlet with mortification, she rolled his handkerchief up into a ball and turned away from him. He had guessed that she thought he was going to kiss her? Why on earth had she thought that? Since he had announced that they were to marry he had made no attempt to touch her in any way at all. She knew how he felt about her and yet here she was quivering with nerves and tension simply because she had quite erroneously thought she glimpsed a hot spark of desire in his eyes.

If he knew, no doubt his contempt would crucify her. By rights she ought to loathe the very thought of him touching her when she knew how little he wanted her, but when were emotions ever governed by logic? Right now there was nothing she wanted more than for him to open his arms to her and to settle her aching head against his shoulder. She ached for the security of his arms round her, protecting her from all her fears and dreads of this new life he was taking her to.

If he really had been taking her home as his new bride she would have been deluging him with questions now, demanding to know as much as he could tell her about the life they would live together. As it was . . .

'I realise you haven't the slightest interest in either me or my family.' The harshly cynical voice drew her attention, her eyes fastening on his as Saul continued curtly, 'But I suggest you find a way of manufacturing some before we arrive in Florida, otherwise my mother is going to be extremely suspicious.'

'You could always tell her the truth.'

She saw him frown. 'She has enough to worry about with my stepfather's health, without me giving her more problems. As far as my parents are concerned, Lucy, our marriage is a perfectly normal one, entered into for all the normal reasons, and I intend that they shall go on thinking that.'

Briefly Lucy envied his mother. He must love her an awful lot to want to protect her from the reality of their marriage. If she had a son, would he love her with the same intensity?

'Surely they'll be surprised that we . . . that we got married so quickly and . . .'

'Not really; they know . . . They know you're carrying my child,' he told her calmly, and yet as he looked away from her Lucy felt sure that he had been about to say something else. Knowing that there was little point in questioning him about it she said instead, 'I suppose they were very shocked.'

'Surprised rather than shocked.'

He gave her a mocking smile as he felt her turn slightly towards him in query.

'My mother is a woman of the world, Lucy, and I'm not a boy any more. Although she's hardly likely to say so, I feel sure that she will be rather surprised that I was careless enough to allow such a situation to arise.'

One eyebrow rose as he looked at her, watching the tide of colour burn up under her skin.

'Never mind,' he taunted softly. 'If she sees you blushing like that, no doubt she'll simply assume I got carried away on a fatal tide of passion.'

Of course Saul must have been involved with other women and of course his mother would know that he did not live like a monk, but would she ever believe that Saul, so controlled, could have behaved in such a reckless way?

All brides must dread meeting an unknown mother-in-law, Lucy reflected, but in her case her anxiety was intensified by the fact that Saul's mother was also her aunt, and in addition there was a history of family enmity between her father and his sister. In the circumstances she could hardly expect Saul's mother to welcome her with open arms.

She shivered.

'Are you feeling all right?'

Saul sounded curt, probably dreading the embarrassment of calling a stewardess over to her, Lucy thought, remembering how angry her father used to get with her when she was a child if she did anything to call attention to herself.

'I'm fine.'

It was the truth. Physically at least she felt reasonably well. The vitamin supplements she was taking were already helping to alleviate the draining exhaustion of her early pregnancy and every day she regained a little more of her own strength.

The flight was a long one and after lunch Lucy gave in to her desire to sleep, turning her head away from Saul. Which made it all the more embarrassing that she should wake up with her head pillowed against his shoulder, his arm curled around her.

To anyone who didn't know the real situation they must look like a devoted couple, she thought as she sat up and Saul immediately removed his arm.

'Sorry about that.'

Her voice sounded stiff with defensiveness as she pulled away.

'Why? Because I'm not Summers?'

Saul's voice was unwarrantedly harsh. Why did he keep having to bring Neville into their conversations? Was he doing it to hurt her? Deliberately mentioning the name of the man he thought she loved to cause her pain? It hurt to know that he thought her capable of making love with him for calculating motives, in order to help Neville. Surely he must have known when he held her in his arms that her emotions were real and not assumed? But why should he care either way? He had made it plain that he had simply been using her as he thought she had been using him.

After that she couldn't sleep again, growing increasingly tense and nervous as the end of their journey drew nearer.

How would she fit in with Saul's family? How much would they be expected to see of them? Where did Saul live? Did he have his own house, or . . .

Almost as though he followed her train of thought he said abruptly, 'Tonight we'll be staying with my parents. They think this is a love-match, Lucy, and I'd be obliged if you don't do anything to alter that impression. I owe my stepfather a good deal,' he added harshly, 'and if you do anything, anything at all to prejudice his health . . .'

What sort of a woman did he think she was? She felt almost sick with despair.

'You don't have to extract promises from me, or make threats, Saul,' she told him tightly. 'I'm as anxious for your family to believe we're happily married as you are.'

She saw his expression and told him tonelessly, 'Our child will be growing up among them. I don't want him to be considered an outcast, to hear gossip about his parents, or . . .

'Him?' Saul queried mockingly, his expression lightening briefly. 'Are you so convinced we will have a son, then?'

Was she? She examined the question and found she didn't really mind if she had a boy or a girl.

' "He" just came automatically,' she told him. The brief softening in his mood encouraged her to ask tentatively, 'Where will we live Saul? Do you . . .'

'At the moment I have an apartment—it's in the centre of town and convenient for my work, but I shall sell it and find something more suited to family life. I spent several years cooped up in an apartment as a child, and it's not what I want for any son or daughter of my own.' He frowned as he said, 'My mother will probably ask us to stay but in the circumstances I think we'd be better using the apartment until we can find the right house. It would be too much of a strain if we had to keep up the pretence of our marriage on a day-to-day basis.'

'Yes.' Oddly enough it made her feel closer to him to hear him say that he, too, was aware of that strain; it made him seem more human, more like the Saul she had seen so briefly in those halcyon days before their quarrel.

'I warn you, you'll be subjected to a good deal of cross questioning by my stepsisters; they both live locally with their families and . . .'

'And quite naturally they're going to be curious about the woman who's married their little brother?' Lucy supplied.

The voice of the captain announced that they were nearing the end of their journey and further personal conversation became impossible in the hurly-burly and bustle of preparations for quitting the plane.

It was not so much the heat as the humidity that struck Lucy first, hitting her like a wall of hot, moist air the moment they left the terminal building. Saul had refused to allow her to help him with their luggage, and now she felt glad. The effect of the humidity was such that it drained her completely of energy.

'Saul! Saul, over here . . .'

A tall, dark-haired woman was waving to them, and Lucy felt her heart jump and then almost stand still as she recognised in his mother her resemblance both to Saul and to her own father.

So this was Saul's mother ... her aunt. Tanned and slim, she was elegantly dressed in walking shorts and a patterned top, her hair elegantly styled, her fingernails gleaming with polish. Against her Lucy felt untidy and drab, conscious of the fact that her hair was probably curling in the humidity and her nose shining. And then, as she was unexpectedly enveloped in a warm hug, she saw past the elegant façade to the woman beyond, and a tiny glimmer of hope began to grow inside her. Saul's mother didn't dislike or resent her.

She was released and held at arm's length, to be studied by twinkling grey eyes, very like Saul's.

'A true Martin by the looks of you, Lucy. That must have pleased your father.' A faint shadow crossed the grey eyes.

'For all that we didn't see eye to eye, I would have come to his funeral if Harry hadn't been so ill. I hated missing it. He was my brother, after all.

'What on earth are you going to call me?' Suddenly she was more practical, as she teased, 'I don't suppose many girls get their aunt as their mother-in-law. Perhaps you should just call me Sophy as Harry's girls do?'

'Save the chit chat for later, Ma,' Saul advised, coming between them to soften his words by kissing her on the cheeks. 'Lucy isn't used to our humidity yet, and she'll probably pass out on us if we leave her standing out here much longer.'

His mother was instantly apologetic. 'Lucy, forgive me, in all the excitement I forgot. Yes,

you do look dreadfully pale you poor thing.
Saul's told me about the baby . . .' Her smile was
warmly encouraging. 'I admit at first I was
somewhat surprised—Saul isn't normally so
unorthodox—but after all what could be nicer
than getting a niece, a daughter-in-law and a
grandchild all at once?'

Chatting away she led the way to her car,
smoothing over Lucy's embarrassment and dis-
comfort, making her feel as though she was
indeed very welcome. It went a long way to
offsetting the anxiety she had endured during the
flight, and as she got into the car Lucy could
almost feel the tension draining out of her.

Saul's mother drove with a competence Lucy
envied when she studied the heavy traffic,
explaining as she drove that their home was
several miles away in a small new township near
the coast.

The car's air-conditioning was blessedly cool
after the heat of the airport.

'How's Harry?' Saul questioned his mother as
they left the freeway and turned on to a more
minor road.

'Better, but fretting to get back to work—you
know what he's like. Dr Schlinder's told him he
must rest and build up his strength before they
can operate.'

She turned to Lucy and said soberly, 'Harry,
my husband, has a problem with two heart
valves. He will be having an operation to replace
them but Matt Schlinder, our doctor, believes in
getting his patients just as fit as he can before
putting them in for surgery, and Harry doesn't

have a lot of patience, I'm afraid. Saul being away has made things worse—Saul's just about the only person he trusts to handle his business affairs properly, which was why he had to come rushing back over here.

'There were problems on one of the construction sites, and it was heading for a real labour confrontation. Harry was worrying so much I was afraid he would have a relapse. I'm sorry I had to drag Saul away from you like that, virtually in the middle of the night.' She turned to her son and said affectionately, 'It was lucky you were able to get that early morning flight, Saul. I was really beginning to panic.'

Lucy glanced across at her husband. He was frowning slightly as he looked out of the window. She hadn't realised he had left the Manor so hurriedly—was that why he hadn't contacted her? Could he have been called away that same night that they had made love? Hope clutched tightly at her stomach and then faded away to make room for pain as she remembered that even if by some coincidence Saul had been called away that night he could always have telephoned her, or written to her. He could even have contacted her on his return ... But no, if she hadn't gone up to the Manor and accidentally bumped into him, she doubted that she would ever have seen him again.

'Nearly there,' Saul's mother commented, mistaking her unhappy silence for tiredness.

'I've told the girls definitely no visitors tonight,' she added, smiling at Lucy. 'They're dying to meet you.' She looked past Lucy to grin at her son. 'Meryl says you've won her twenty dollars. Apparently she bet Christie that much twelve years ago, when you first went over to England, that you'd fallen for Lucy, and now she claims she was right. You'll find my stepdaughters are inclined to be rather outspoken,' she told Lucy. 'An American habit that I still find startling at times. They accuse me of being too British and "buttoned-up" and claim that I've brought Saul up the same way, which is why he's chosen to marry a British girl.'

They were driving through a new township now, and Lucy looked around with interest, wondering if this was the sort of place where she and Saul would eventually make their home.

As yet she had barely thought beyond the initial stages of their marriage, but now she had a bleak picture of the years ahead, empty of love and warmth, and she had to close her eyes against the tears prickling her eyelids.

'Nearly there.'

Sophy Bradford turned off the main road into one lined with grass verges and trees, with large houses set well back from it on both sides.

She turned into the drive of one of them, activating the automatic gates. Trees and shrubs hid the house from view, but, as they drove past well-tended flower beds and lawns, Lucy recognised the expensive gloss of wealth and good taste.

The house was long and low, its walls white, and embellished with delicate iron grilles and balconies.

'This place was built in the thirties by a wealthy bootlegger. We bought it five years ago when Harry first retired from the business. It's too large for us really, but neither of us likes cramped surroundings.' She stopped in front of the house and, as they got out of the car the main door was opened by a smiling Mexican maid.

'This is Elena,' Sophy told her, introducing the maid. 'She and her husband, Tomás, run the house for us. Come on in. Is my husband in his study?' she asked the maid as Lucy and Saul followed her inside.

'No, I'm here.'

Harry Bradford was not much taller than his wife, his skin tanned and seamed by years of exposure to the elements, his hair grey. He looked frail, Lucy thought as she stepped forward to be introduced to him, but as she recognised the integrity and astuteness in his eyes she realised why Saul was so fond of him. Instinctively she knew she was in the presence of a man who lived his life by a strict code of ethics. Here was a man who was probably a little old-fashioned in his attitude towards her sex, but who would always treat people with consideration and respect.

'So this is the girl who finally brought you down, eh, Saul? You're very welcome here, my dear,' he told Lucy. 'Very welcome indeed. I've been telling this young hell-raiser for years that it's high time he settled down.'

'We'll have dinner in an hour, Elena,' Sophy told the maid. 'Would you ask Tomás to take the bags to the guest suite?'

'You'll want to shower and change before we eat,' Sophy told Lucy. 'I'll show you to your room while these two catch up on business.'

*   *   *

The guest suite was at the far end of the house overlooking beautifully tended lawns and flower beds.

'The pool area is over there to the right,' Sophy told Lucy, as she stood next to her in front of the french windows of an attractively furnished private sitting-room. 'And beyond it is the tennis court. Do you play?'

'Not much,' Lucy confessed. 'Although I was keen on it at school.'

'Well it's the latest craze around here. Anyone who's anyone belongs to one or other of the local clubs; most of my contemporaries have private coaching as well. Of course you won't be wanting to involve yourself in any sports at the moment, but later . . . after the baby arrives . . .

'The business takes Saul away quite a lot, visiting the various construction sites, and you'll find it helpful to have a circle of friends of your own. When you eventually find a house, I recommend you join the local country club. It takes a while to make the adjustment from the English way of life to the American—I know. But don't fall into the trap that I did, of isolating yourself completely from everyone. My first husband had to travel a great deal, and I was on my own with Saul when he did. I found I became very lonely. Of course I know you'll have your writing, but that is a very solitary occupation.'

Sophy's advice was sound and practical, and it warmed Lucy's heart that Saul's mother should be concerned for her well-being.

'Saul's told us about the problem with your

pregnancy,' she commented as she turned away from the window and walked over to another door. 'This is the bedroom,' she said as she opened it and waited for Lucy to walk through.

Like the sitting-room, the bedroom was decorated in soft yellows and blues, the floral fabric very English country-house in style, and the walls washed in a soft golden yellow and rag-rolled.

'Anything British is very "in" over here at the moment,' Sophy commented. 'But I must admit it was more nostalgia than fashion that made me have this suite decorated like this.'

'It's lovely,' Lucy told her, looking hurriedly away from the huge double bed. Seeing it had given her a shock. She knew that Saul's family were not aware of the reality of their marriage, but somehow she had expected that they would be given a room with two single beds.

'The bathroom's through here,' Sophy told her, indicating a door in the far wall of the bedroom, 'and the closet's there. Since you're only staying the one night, I'll tell Elena not to unpack your things. Saul says you'll be living in his apartment until you can find somewhere more congenial. The girls will be coming round for lunch tomorrow, so you'll get a chance to meet them then. I'll leave you to get changed now.'

Before she left, Sophy turned to kiss her cheek. She squeezed her arm lightly as she released her. 'I'm very glad that Saul married you, Lucy,' she told her, frowning slightly as she saw the sparkle of tears in the brown eyes. 'My dear, is something wrong? Don't you feel well?'

'I'm fine ... Just overwhelmed by your kindness,' Lucy told her shakily. 'I thought you'd probably loathe me, especially when I think of the way my father behaved towards Saul.'

'George was my brother, don't forget,' Sophy reminded her drily. 'I know exactly what he was like; we never saw eye to eye as children. I liked your mother very much though. She was a sweet girl.' She frowned and then said honestly, 'I must say I was angry when I heard what George had done with the estate—but I suppose I should have expected it. He always was almost obsessive about it. He must have been bitterly disappointed when his second marriage produced another daughter.'

Lucy was beginning to feel the effects of the long flight; exhaustion creeping over her and Saul's mother's warm reception of her relaxing her normal guard, she replied without thinking, 'Oh yes, especially with Oliver being born before he and Fanny ...' As she realised what she was saying she went silent, a dark tide of guilty colour stealing up under her skin.

Sophy frowned again, and then said slowly, 'Are you saying that Oliver is George's child?'

She had said too much to retract now and, biting her lip, Lucy nodded her head. 'That was why he sold off so much of the estate. He wanted to provide for Oliver. He wanted to have him made legitimate so that he could inherit but Fanny wouldn't hear of it. She went frantic at the very suggestion because she said she couldn't endure the gossip it would lead to. I don't think she ever really understood my father's obsession for the Manor. She could see no real advantage in

Oliver inheriting it, especially when my father had provided so well for him financially.'

'If Oliver had been legitimate, would he have been able to keep the Manor going—financially I mean?'

'No,' Lucy told her honestly. 'And I think in his heart my father knew that. If he himself had lived much longer he would have had to sell—either that or let the house deteriorate around him. The estimate for the roof repairs alone was nearly £250,000, more than my father realised from everything he sold.'

'Saul intends to keep it—and to have it fully restored. He can afford to of course. Thanks to my husband Saul's a very, very wealthy man. Harry gave both girls a million dollars when they married but Saul is his partner in the business. Those two are much on the same wavelength when it comes to the construction industry, and they're very close—much closer in many ways than if they were actually father and son.

'I'm glad Saul found you, Lucy. We've been worried about him; wanting to see him settling down with a wife and family and yet worried that he might marry the wrong girl. He's had lots of girlfriends—even several serious relationships—but I think this is the first time I've ever seen him genuinely in love. I could tell when he came home when Harry was ill that he wasn't really with us, but of course we already knew about you from his letters and phone calls.

'I'll leave you now,' Sophy said with a smile. 'If I stay here much longer it will be dinner time and neither of us will be ready.'

Alone in the suite, Lucy went to stare out of the window, turning only when Tomás came in with their cases, which he put in the bedroom. It had surprised her to hear that Saul had talked about her to his family. If all he had intended all along was simply to pay her back for her childish cruelty all those years ago, surely he would have kept quiet about her. But perhaps because of their blood relationship his mother had been curious about her? Telling herself that such speculation would do nothing but re-activate hopes she already knew were pointless, Lucy searched through her case for the silk dress she intended to wear for dinner, noting with relief that it was not creased, and taking it and fresh underwear with her into the bathroom.

She was dressed and putting on her make-up when Saul came into the suite.

'I didn't unpack your case because I wasn't sure what you'd want,' she told him, watching him unfasten and then flick back its lid.

When he selected a white tuxedo and dark trousers, she knew she had been right in thinking his parents would dine in some formality.

Physically they made a well-matched couple, she thought miserably half an hour later as she caught a glimpse of their double reflection in the bedroom mirror, but they weren't a couple at all—at least not in the true sense of the word. Just two people held together by the demands and responsibility of the new life they had so thoughtlessly conceived.

The conversation over dinner was light and entertaining, her mother-in-law an experienced and skilled hostess. Never for one moment did Lucy feel out of place or unwanted. Her pregnancy was mentioned a couple of times in the context of the general conversation, Sophy so patently relaxed about it that Lucy felt some of her own apprehensions ease.

She was grateful when Sophy suggested an early night, knowing that it was only will-power that had kept her from yawning openly over the last stages of the meal.

Suspecting that Saul would probably remain with his parents, she excused herself, returning Sophy's almost motherly kiss as she and Harry said their 'good nights'.

As she walked past Saul's chair, she smiled at him, too, trying not to show how tense she was.

'I won't be long,' he told her. 'I'm rather tired myself.'

While Harry laughed and teased him for being very unromantic for a newly married man, Lucy made her escape.

Already she was beginning to take the air-conditioning for granted, showering quickly, and then cleansing her face and brushing her hair before slipping between deliciously cool and soft percale sheets. The quality of the bedding was something she had already noted and decided to ask her mother-in-law about. There were a lot of adjustments she was going to have to make in her new life and she was glad that Sophy was there to help and advise her. At home they used linen sheets, originally bought by her great-grand-mother, and still going strong, but they were nothing like as soft and comfortable as these.

The sound of a door opening and then closing brought her up through several layers of sleep but not fully awake. The alarm the sounds had triggered off faded as her subconscious recognised the sounds of the decisive masculine movements about the room. The shower ran, a distantly heard and faintly comforting sound. There were movements and then the sensation of the bed depressing, accompanied by the silken rustle of sheets and an elusively familiar, tangy male scent. Instinctively, Lucy turned towards the source of it, her sleep deepening into complete relaxation as she snuggled up against the warm male body so close to her own. A smile curved her mouth as she nuzzled, contentedly, deeper into the secure warmth.

Lying on his side looking down at her, Saul tensed and swore silently, reaching out to push her away, and then changing his mind and instead settling her more comfortably against his body, his arm curling around her.

CHAPTER TEN

LUCY was having a dream. In her dream she was in Saul's arms, and he was making love to her as he had done before that fatal quarrel. Wherever he touched her skin tiny *frissons* of pleasure burned along her nerve endings. What he was doing to her was delightful, but she yearned and ached for more. She reached out towards him, wanting to convey with her own touch how much she wanted him. Her fingers touched smooth skin and hard muscle. The layers of sleep parted abruptly, the sensation of flesh and bone beneath her fingers too real to be the product of any mere dream. Panic fluttered inside her as her eyes opened. She was lying in Saul's arms, the pre-drawn light filtering through the room.

Like a guilty child she snatched her fingers away from his skin, her throat suddenly almost too tight for her to breathe. What was she doing?

In the same instant that she came awake she realised that Saul was completely naked, the fragile silk of her nightdress the only barrier between them. Filled with panic she tried to wriggle away, dreading the thought of him waking up and finding her here in his arms, but the minute she tried to move the arm round her waist tightened, his eyelids opening to reveal darkly glittering and far too alert eyes.

'Let me go! What are you doing?' The words tumbled from her lips with feverish panic.

'You tell me. You were the one who started this,' he told her mockingly, 'snuggling up to me like a little kitten begging to be stroked.'

The picture his words were making was too intimate . . . it made her too vulnerable. Hot colour stormed her skin as she listened to him. Had she really? She swallowed hard and forced herself to meet his eyes.

'Think I'm lying?' he asked softly.

Why should he? He didn't want her, while she . . .

Numbly she shook her head, and then said huskily, 'I'm sorry, I . . .'

'Don't be.' His voice was oddly harsh as he added, 'I'm still man enough to enjoy having a beautiful woman cuddle up to me—even if she is asleep.'

He was smiling, Lucy realised incredulously, almost laughing in fact, his grey eyes gleaming, not with dislike or contempt, but amusement and . . . Her breath caught, her throat muscles rigid as she recognised the hot glitter of desire in them.

'Of course, I'd enjoy it much more if you weren't wearing this,' he murmured against her ear, his fingers on the bow-tied shoulder straps of her nightgown.

She really ought to move away from him; she knew that, but he had already untied the bows and her heart was thudding so hard she thought it might well break through her ribs, especially now that his hand was resting against it.

'Lucy . . .'

Her tongue touched her dry upper lip as she caught the fevered undertone of arousal hoarsening his voice.

'Don't do that!' He was looking at her mouth, and obediently, as though she had no will of her own, her tongue retreated.

It was like a dream, everything totally unreal, especially the unmistakable tremor in his hands as they locked on her now bare shoulders, his tongue touching the still dry tension of her mouth, stroking, moistening, totally capturing her senses until she moaned softly under her need to feel his mouth against her own, reaching up to tug his head downwards, her fingers curling into the thick tousled hair, her face lifting eagerly towards him as she shuddered beneath the fierce onslaught of his kiss.

Since she was quite well aware that Saul would never, ever kiss her with this starving hunger, there was no need for her to try and rationalise anything. This was not reality; it could not be, and hence there was no need for her to resist or fight it—or to conceal her feelings, her need and love that welled up inside her, finding expression in the trembling softness of her body against his as her lips parted eagerly to the fierce thrust of his tongue.

His hands swept upwards, his fingers gentle on the vulnerable contours of her throat and then fiercely locking in her hair, tightening against her scalp as desire flowed between them fuelled by the hot urgency of their mouths.

Still kissing her, Saul thrust aside the bedclothes, and instinctively she moved towards him, welcoming the weight of his body against her own, her nipples hardening into taut desire as they pushed protestingly against the fine silk that separated them.

When Saul wrenched his mouth from her own, Lucy felt so totally bereft that she wanted to cry. She reached for him, her hands encountering only the thick silkiness of his hair, her fingers clenching convulsively into his scalp as his head cupped her breast, his mouth tugging feverishly at its swollen crest, too hungry for her to wait until he had pushed aside the fine silk.

Her heart thumped frantically, her body arching in a delirium of remembered pleasure.

'Lucy.'

His head lay against her breast, the wet silk clinging to her skin. Caught up in the fever of her own arousal Lucy recognised the thick drugging quality of his desire. His voice was raw with it, as unfamiliar to her as the shudders that convulsed his body.

'I shouldn't be doing this.'

The words were hoarse with self-imposed restraint, his body hard and aroused against her own. He wanted her, Lucy thought frantically. He did want her, no matter what he might say, and she wanted him. The fact that she could arouse him to physical desire gave her new hope. Perhaps after all something could be salvaged, something made of their marriage. Perhaps if she told him the truth about Neville . . .

Despite what he had said, he hadn't moved, and now he bent again towards her body, his lips gently caressing the fullness of her breast, as though unable to resist their temptation. Shivers of pleasure rippled through her, drowning her in waves of fire.

When she could find her breath she gasped achingly, 'If it's because of Neville . . .'

'Damn Neville!' Saul swore violently, releasing her. 'You're married to me, not him. He doesn't want you, Lucy. Not the way I do.' He broke off and added thickly, 'I was thinking about the baby . . . The doctor . . .'

The doctor had in fact tactfully informed her that there was no reason why she should not lead a perfectly normal married life, at least until the later stages of her pregnancy, but it was not this that made Lucy's eyes widen slowly. Saul had said he wanted her . . .

'You want me.' She repeated the words slowly, savouring them, looking down at him as his head lifted.

'I know I'm the first man to make love to you, but you're not that naïve, Lucy,' he told her roughly. 'You know damn well what you do to me.' His glance skimmed the outline of their entwined bodies, and Lucy felt her skin grow hot as it lingered meaningfully on the place where his body throbbed its message of desire and need against her own.

'Did you really want me before . . . when you threw me out?' It was a question that pride should have prevented her from asking, but now the words were out and could not be recalled.

Saul was frowning, moving slightly away from her, so that she instinctively sought to close that tiny gap. Still frowning he let her, watching her eyes close as her body absorbed the pleasure of being close to him.

'You know I did,' he said flatly. 'Do you honestly think I could have made love to you the way I did simply out of . . .'

'Revenge? I thought you must have done,' she said quietly, watching the incredulous disbelief fill his eyes.

'Revenge?' His eyes narrowed thoughtfully, and he said with probing softness, 'I was half mad with jealousy, Lucy; surely you realised that the moment I mentioned Summers' name?'

'No,' Lucy said slowly, 'I thought your making love to me must all be part of some plan you'd conceived to punish me for . . . for everything.'

Frowning, he sat up facing her; the pre-dawn light was fading now and Lucy blinked as he reached out to snap on one of the bedside lamps. Its golden glow encompassed them both, emphasising the deep tan of his skin and the paleness of hers.

'I think you and I have some talking to do,' Saul said softly. 'Just tell me one thing. What does Neville Summers mean to you?'

'Nothing,' Lucy told him promptly. 'I've already told you that before. He's my cousin, and I'm very, very fond of his parents, but I saw Neville as he really is years ago.' She had said more than she ever intended, but suddenly it didn't matter what she might betray to Saul; instinct told her that having said so much she might as well go on.

'When he came to see me that afternoon, to try

and blackmail me into giving him some help, my first instinct was to refuse outright, but I knew if I did he wouldn't tell me any more, whereas if I pretended I would help, I could learn more about his plans.'

'But when I asked you if you had had any visitors, you denied it,' Saul reminded her.

'Because you seemed so worried ... I didn't want to add to your problems. I told you that then.'

'Yes, you did,' he agreed sombrely, 'and I was so caught up in my own destructive jealousy I didn't know what to believe. All I could think about was that summer and how he had encouraged you to reject me. And how much he had enjoyed it. He knew then that I was attracted to you, Lucy, even if you didn't. He even taunted me with it.' He smiled derisively as he saw the disbelief in her eyes. 'Oh yes, he knew all right.'

'I thought it might be something like that ... that it could be because you were jealous of him that you had ... that you rejected me.'

'You did some pretty definite rejecting of your own,' Saul reminded her. 'You let me think you were in league with him against me.'

'Because I was so hurt that you could ... that you could make love to me like that and then reject me. I had to have some means of self-defence.'

'Lucy ...' He pulled her gently towards him, resting her head against his shoulder. 'Is it too late for us to start again? To try and build on what we *do* have? We desire each other.'

'Desire isn't love.' She said it unhappily, unable to look at him.

'No,' he agreed after some hesitation. 'But while one of us loves, surely . . .'

Lucy stiffened, wrenching herself out of his arms. So all along he *had* known how she felt about him.

'All right, I admit I do love you, Saul,' she agreed, trembling with emotion and temper, 'but . . .'

'Hey, wait a minute. What do you mean, "you admit you love me"?'

'Exactly what I said,' she snapped back, hating the smile that curled his mouth and brought glimmering sparks of delight to his eyes. 'You've obviously known all along how I felt, and I . . .'

He was shaking his head, his smile going. 'No, Lucy,' he said seriously, 'I haven't known. Why the devil do you think I was so jealous of Neville? So unsure of you? Not because I knew you loved me, for sure.'

'But you said . . .' Her forehead crinkled into a small frown.

'What I said was, as long as one of us loves . . . But the one I was referring to was me, not you.'

For several seconds she was stupefied into silence and then she objected shakily,

'But you can't love me. You left without a word, and never even tried to get in touch with me. If we hadn't met by accident at the Manor, you'd . . .'

'I'd have torn England apart trying to find you,' he groaned suddenly, pulling her into his arms, his voice thick and raw with emotion as he told her.

'I was just setting out for the Dower House

that night to see you and apologise when my mother rang. She was in such a panic about Harry, I didn't dare take the time to talk to you about my jealousy. I wasn't sure enough of you to think you would readily understand. I'd been shocked by my behaviour—shocked and disgusted, and I knew you would be, too. It wasn't something that could be put right in a phone call or a letter. I'd hoped to get back sooner than I did, and when I did manage to fly in it was to find that you'd left. It was like a blow in the gut. I took it to mean that you were finished with me . . . That I'd been right after all and Neville was the one you wanted. I can't begin to tell you what it did to me to think that all the time I was making love to you, you were wishing it was someone else. It just tore me apart.

'I swore I didn't want anything else to do with you, that I was better off without you . . . but none of it worked. And then, when your uncle got in touch with me to tell me about the baby . . .'

He saw her start of shock and smiled grimly.

'Apparently he got my number from Patterson, and he told me everything; everything apart from the fact that you loved me, that is. You were carrying my child . . . That made you both my responsibility. I knew then what I was going to do. I told myself I was only marrying you because of the baby, but I knew damn well that wasn't it. It was no accident that I was at the Manor that morning. I'd flown over the night before determined not to let you out of my sight until you'd agreed to marry me. Believe me,

Lucy, if it hadn't been for Harry's illness you'd
have been back in my arms before dawn that
morning, hearing how much I loved and wanted
you.'

It was said with too much conviction to be a
lie, and anyway what would be the point?

'You really love me?'

She said it uncertainly, like a child promised
something so magnificent that it hardly dared
believe the promise was real.

'You'd better believe it,' Saul told her wryly.
'I'm surprised you haven't already heard as much
from my mother. I told her a long time ago that
I'd found the girl I wanted to spend my life
with.'

'A long time ago?' Her eyebrows lifted as she
teased him. 'We've only known each other a few
months.'

'Correction,' Saul whispered against her
mouth, 'I knew you twelve years ago.'

He felt the shock of surprise ripple through her
body.

'I fell pretty hard for you that summer, Lucy,
and though what I felt faded over the years, it
never went away completely. When your father
died and I knew I'd inherited, I was in two minds
about coming over. I told myself it was safer not
to, but I couldn't forget that all those years ago
I'd sensed that beneath the teenage disdain you'd
shown me was someone very different. And then
I heard from Patterson about what your father
had done to the estate, and I told myself I was
wrong after all . . . But still I had to come and
find out for myself.'

There would be time later to tell him the truth about Oliver. Right now all she wanted was to be held like this in his arms, his mouth moving with tantalising slowness over her skin, his hands sliding the silk of her nightdress from her body, his earlier urgency gone as he started to make love to her with a slow languor that her body loved.

'Let's start again,' he murmured against her mouth, teasing it with small biting kisses. 'Right from the moment when we walked into my bedroom.'

He tensed as Lucy shook her head, levering himself away from her body slightly. Her heart jolted against her ribs as she saw the uncertainty in his eyes and knew his vulnerability.

'If we do that I'll be losing my most treasured memories,' she told him softly. 'Not to mention this.' She patted her stomach, her breath suspended as she saw his eyes darken and burn with passion.

'If you say so.' His voice was thick and slurred. 'But I'll give you other memories, Lucy, lots and lots of them.'

'I thought you were angry because I was a virgin,' she told him dreamily, gasping softly as his mouth slid down her throat, teasing the tender skin. 'That you felt it trapped you into a more serious relationship than you'd wanted.'

'No . . . If I seemed angry it was because I felt you must really love Summers so much that you hadn't been able to give yourself to anyone else. I knew he didn't love you, you see, and I thought you'd decided that I would be as good a

substitute as anyone ... That when I touched
and caressed you, you were thinking of him.'

His mouth had found her breast and was
caressing the swollen, wanton peak with a skill
that threatened to drive her out of her mind.

Shudders of pleasure rippled through her,
languor forgotten in the swift upsurge of desire,
her body abandoning restraint as it moved
eagerly against Saul's, inviting his possession.

Later, their bodies sleepily entwined, they
talked with the freedom that only lovers know,
sleeping and then waking in the brilliant early
morning sunlight to make love again.

'I could stay here like this all day,' Lucy
murmured happily, her lips caressing the smooth
skin of his shoulder.

'I only wish we could.' Saul's smile was rueful.
'I thought by staying with my parents, I was
removing myself from temptation. I fully
intended to be out of here this morning long
before you woke up, but I hadn't allowed for the
effect on my will-power of having you cuddle
into my arms and wrap yourself round my body.'

'Ah, so it's all my fault is it?' Lucy teased.

Happiness filled her, making her feel as light-
headed and giddy as a child.

'It's always the woman's fault,' Saul told her
smugly, dodging the mock blow she aimed at him
and trapping her in his arms.

'Well, well, you've surfaced at long last.'

Hand in hand they strolled towards the group
sitting by the pool. The woman who had called
out to them got up, two toddlers at her side.

'I do believe you're blushing, brother dear,' she said with a grin as she came towards him. 'Christie, you most definitely do owe me that twenty dollars.' She had reached them now and her smile for Lucy was warm and slightly mischievous.

'Lucy, come and tell us all about how you managed to hook this marriage-shy guy,' she invited her new stepsister-in-law, but it was Saul who answered her, his laconic voice at odds with the slumberous passion in his eyes as he responded, looking at Lucy.

'Quite simply, my dear sister, it's called love.'

The way he looked at her made her body tremble and wish they were still alone, but then one of the children piped up shrilly, and the spell was broken; Sophy came forward to lead Lucy to a comfortable chair, Saul went over to talk to Harry and his brothers-in-law.

So began the pattern of her new life, Lucy thought as she sat down, and from it she would weave a warm and protective cloth, but the strongest thread would always be the one linking her to Saul; the thread that represented their love.

'Tell us all about this Manor,' Christie invited. 'We're all dying to go over and see it.'

Obediently she began to talk, and then, as though responding to something she alone could hear, she turned her head. Saul was smiling at her. She smiled back, knowing that like her he was waiting for the time when they could be alone.

'Come on you two love birds,' Christie teased. 'Break it up, otherwise you'll be making us old married folks jealous.'

Across the sunlit space Lucy's eyes met Saul's, her body quivering in response to the memory of his hands touching it. She loved and was loved in return. Life could hold no gift she would cherish more.

Merry Christmas one and all.

CHANCES ARE *Barbara Delinsky*	THE GIFT OF HAPPINESS *Amanda Carpenter*
ONE ON ONE *Jenna Lee Joyce*	HAWK'S PREY *Carole Mortimer*
AN IMPRACTICAL PASSION *Vicki Lewis Thompson*	TWO WEEKS TO REMEMBER *Betty Neels*
A WEEK FROM FRIDAY *Georgia Bockoven*	YESTERDAY'S MIRROR *Sophie Weston*

More choice for the Christmas stocking. Two special reading packs from Mills & Boon. Adding more than a touch of romance to the festive season.

AVAILABLE: OCTOBER, 1986   PACK PRICE: £4.80   Mills & Boon

Mills & Boon

YOU'RE INVITED TO ACCEPT **FOUR ROMANCES** AND A TOTE BAG **FREE!**

Acceptance card

| NO STAMP NEEDED | Post to: Reader Service, FREEPOST, P.O. Box 236, Croydon, Surrey. CR9 9EL |

YES! Please send me 4 free Mills & Boon Romances and my free tote bag – and reserve a Reader Service Subscription for me. If I decide to subscribe I shall receive 6 new Romances every month as soon as they come off the presses for £7.20 together with a FREE monthly newsletter including information on top authors and special offers, exclusively for Reader Service subscribers. There are no postage and packing charges, and I understand I may cancel or suspend my subscription at any time. If I decide not to subscribe I shall write to you within 10 days. Even if I decide not to subscribe the 4 free novels and the tote bag are mine to keep forever. I am over 18 years of age   EP20R

NAME _____

(CAPITALS PLEASE)

ADDRESS _____

_____

_____ **POSTCODE** _____

From the author of Gypsy comes a spellbinding romance.

Unresistingly drawn into Rand's arms, Merlyn then had to suffer his rejection, as he retreated into his own private torment where he still grieved the loss of his beautiful and talented wife, Suzie.

How would Merlyn then persuade him that she would be right to play Suzie in a film based on the actress's life?

It took an unseen hand to make Rand aware of Merlyn's own special kind of magic.

ANOTHER BESTSELLER FROM CAROLE MORTIMER

WORLDWIDE

AVAILABLE IN NOVEMBER PRICE £2.50
Available from Boots, Martins, John Menzies, WH Smiths, Woolworth's, and other paperback stockists.